Ali

# NANCY DREW

by Daniela Burr
based on the screenplay by Tiffany Paulsen
and on the characters created by
Carolyn Keene

Simon Spotlight
New York   London   Toronto   Sydney

WARNER BROS. PICTURES PRESENTS
IN ASSOCIATION WITH VIRTUAL STUDIOS A JERRY WEINTRAUB PRODUCTION A FILM BY ANDREW FLEMING "NANCY DREW" EMMA ROBERTS
JOSH FLITTER MAX THIERIOT RACHAEL LEIGH COOK AND TATE DONOVAN COSTUMES DESIGNED BY JEFFREY KURLAND
CO-PRODUCED BY CHERYLANNE MARTIN EDITED BY JEFF FREEMAN, A.C.E. DIRECTOR OF PHOTOGRAPHY ALEXANDER GRUSZYNSKI, A.S.C.
EXECUTIVE PRODUCERS SUSAN EKINS MARK VAHRADIAN BENJAMIN WAISBREN BASED ON CHARACTERS CREATED BY CAROLYN KEENE STORY BY TIFFANY PAULSEN
SCREENPLAY BY ANDREW FLEMING AND TIFFANY PAULSEN PRODUCED BY JERRY WEINTRAUB DIRECTED BY ANDREW FLEMING

VIRTUAL STUDIOS   JW PRODUCTIONS   PG PARENTAL GUIDANCE SUGGESTED   SOME MATERIAL MAY NOT BE SUITABLE FOR CHILDREN   Mild Violence, Thematic Elements And Brief Language   www.nancydrewmovie.com    WARNER BROS. PICTURES ©2007 Warner Bros. Ent. All Rights Reserved

This book is a work of fiction. Any references to historical events, real people, or real locales are used fictitiously. Other names, characters, places, and incidents are the product of the author's imagination, and any resemblance to actual events or locales or persons, living or dead, is entirely coincidental.

Based on the movie *Nancy Drew* by Warner Bros. Entertainment Inc.

SIMON SPOTLIGHT
An imprint of Simon & Schuster Children's Publishing Division
1230 Avenue of the Americas, New York, New York 10020
NANCY DREW © Warner Bros. Entertainment Inc.
NANCY DREW is a trademark of Simon & Schuster, Inc. (s07)
All rights reserved, including the right of reproduction in whole or in part in any form.
SIMON SPOTLIGHT and colophon are registered trademarks of Simon & Schuster, Inc.
Manufactured in the United States of America
First Edition
10 9 8 7 6 5 4 3 2 1
ISBN-13: 978-1-4169-3899-6
ISBN-10: 1-4169-3899-0

# CHAPTER 1

Nancy Drew sat crouched in the small closet in Pastor Murray's office. She didn't dare breathe, never mind move. In the office just beyond the closet, she could hear the voices of two dangerous thieves pulling off a burglary. The situation was extremely dangerous, and keeping her presence unknown for as long as she could was of the utmost importance.

But suddenly the closet door swung open, and a tall muscular man with a dark mustache glared down at her. "Who are you?" he demanded in a harsh, gruff voice.

The pretty teen detective with the beautiful honey brown hair straightened her sweater and then held out her hand. "Hello, I'm Nancy Drew," she said, rising to her feet, demonstrating that she was not at all intimidated by the man's size. "It's nice to meet you. May I ask, who are you?"

The second man, who was even larger and more menacing than his partner, stepped forward. "Guess," he growled.

"All right," Nancy agreed with a grin. "I'm guessing you two are working with Lawrence McNabb, the locksmith, that he gives you the keys, and that you're responsible for the recent string of burglaries. However, you should know that the district attorney is only interested in McNabb—you two could make a deal with him—and that Charlie, the security guard, is about to walk through that door."

A moment later, as if on cue, Charlie entered the room. "Hi," he said, obviously unaware of the dangerous situation he'd just stepped into.

The two burly men exchanged glances. Was it possible that they'd been defeated by a teenage girl and a skinny, bumbling security guard?

Apparently it was, because at that very moment Nancy was using the pastor's desk phone to dial the River Heights Police Department. Naturally her call was put straight through to Chief McGinnis. The chief always took Nancy's calls. She was his best detective—or at least she would be if she were on his staff. Nancy was only an *amateur* detective. But she was an incredibly super sleuth.

"Well, hey there, Nancy," the chief greeted her over the phone. He listened for a moment as Nancy politely asked him what was new. "Oh, not much," he replied. "I got a pair of new rubber waders I'm itching to try out on Sunday. How about you?"

Nancy calmly explained that she was currently in Pastor Murray's office with the two thieves who were doing the dirty work in the McNabb robbery case. At the moment she was fine. But Charlie was a little uncomfortable— what with his having been tied up by the thieves and all.

Nancy spoke to the chief for a few minutes, and then hung up and turned to the two hardened criminals. "We've talked this over," she told them. "Taking me to another location makes it kidnapping. Mandatory minimum: twenty years. Now, I promise to get a deal, so please be patient."

The larger of the thugs, Steve, looked at his partner. "She did promise," he said.

The second man, Gary, nodded his agreement.

A few moments later the squad cars could be heard arriving at the church. Their loud alarms clearly agitated the criminals. They began pacing angrily. Nancy was nervous too, but she kept her cool, just like always. As long as she stayed calm, chances were the burglars would too.

"Listen to me," Nancy explained slowly. "I'll get Pastor Murray to drop the breaking and entering charges if you agree to some kind of counseling. Anger issues don't just go away."

Gary glared at her furiously. "I don't need a shrink!" he barked.

"Yeah you do," Steve told him. He turned to Nancy. "He gets cranky when he hasn't eaten. I told him to have a snack. One summer we were on Fire Island and—"

"Hey!" Gary shouted. "Not that story again!"

It was obvious to Nancy that Gary was getting hungry. And the last thing she wanted was a cranky crook on her hands. She reached into her shoulder bag and fumbled around for a moment.

"What's that?" Gary demanded.

"My sleuth kit," Nancy told him, and she began emptying its contents, looking for something that might calm the situation. "Flashlight, fountain pen, notebook, magnifying glass, fingerprint powder, digital recorder . . ." A smile appeared on her face as she pulled out the perfect thing. "One of Hannah's lemon bars," she said, holding up the small yellow pastry.

"What's that?" Gary was practically salivating.

"That looks delicious," Steve, his equally hungry partner, agreed.

Nancy smiled triumphantly as she split the bar in half and gave one half to each of the men.

While Nancy was making sure that all the sugar levels were kept up inside the pastor's office, Chief McGinnis was outside making sure that everything was ready for a safe arrest of the two burglars. Already his police car, a fire truck, and a photographer from the local newspaper had arrived. A crowd of neighbors and members of the River Heights community had gathered around as well.

A tall, muscular teenager drove up and parked nearby. He burst out of his old truck and pushed his way through the crowd until he found George Fayne and Bess Marvin, Nancy's two closest girlfriends. "Is Nancy okay?" the boy asked them nervously.

Bess smiled at the look of worry on Ned Nickerson's face. It was so obvious that he had a crush on Nancy. "Are you kidding?" she asked him. "She's loving it."

Ned sighed. Nancy's sleuthing always put her in some danger, and she always loved it. However, it made *him* crazy. He needed to talk to her *right away*. Quickly Ned signaled to Chief McGinnis. The police chief nodded and handed the boy his cell phone.

"Nancy?" Ned said into the receiver.

"Hi, Ned," Nancy replied cheerfully.

"So with you going away and all, I think we need to

have a talk about *us*. I had this dream during my nap today that you went to California and met that guy on *Smallville* and you got amnesia, and you literally forgot you ever knew me and then I turned into a squirrel," he blurted out in one breath. "What do you think that means?"

"Um, Ned," Nancy said, glancing at the two angry men and the tied-up security guard who were in the office with her. "Can we talk about this later? I'm just a little busy."

Ned blushed as he caught a glimpse of Bess and George nearby. They were shaking their heads in disbelief. Obviously they'd all heard his big speech—the squirrel thing and all. "Yeah. Sorry." He handed the phone back to the police chief.

"Not appropriate, Ned," George scolded him.

"Do you take naps?" Bess asked, concerned.

Before Ned could answer, Carson Drew came running up to the chief. "What's going on? Is she okay?" he asked, his face ragged with worry about his daughter.

"Don't worry. I just talked to her and she's doing fine," the chief assured Carson.

Mr. Drew stared at the outside of the pastor's office and sighed heavily. He would have to take the chief's word for it. But he certainly wished he could know what was going on inside that building.

Surprisingly, all was calm inside. In fact, the thug with the anger management issue had just agreed to therapy in exchange for Nancy's putting in a good word with the DA. Now they were ready to turn themselves in. As they headed toward the office door, Steve stopped and turned to Nancy.

"I just want to thank you, Nancy Drew," he said sincerely. "I've always heard the nicest things about you, the way you solve mysteries and help people—"

His partner grimaced angrily. "Steve, please don't thank her for turning us in," Gary growled.

"I think Crankenstein needs another lemon bar," Steve replied teasingly. "I thought the Crankesaurus was extinct. I'm so sorry, Cranky Doodle Dandy."

Nancy giggled despite herself, and moved closer to the door. But only Steve walked beside her.

"I can't do this," Gary announced all of a sudden.

"Gary, we made a deal," Steve reminded him.

"*Deals go wrong*," Gary insisted angrily.

Steve turned toward where Nancy had been standing. But the teen crime-stopper had disappeared!

"Hey! Where is she?" Gary demanded. "We need her." He shoved Steve back across the office and through the door that led to the church. "You take that side," he ordered as he began searching behind the pews for a sign of Nancy Drew.

Inside the dimly lit church, Nancy seemed to have literally vanished into thin air. In fact, the only things resembling humans were the white statues of saints that lined one of the church walls.

As Steve walked past the row of statues, he failed to notice that one of them wasn't made of plaster or stone. The smallest of the statues was pure flesh and blood—with a white sweater pulled over her head. Nancy was standing perfectly still, camouflaged among the saints.

But she couldn't stand that still forever, especially not once her nose started to itch. The second after Steve passed by, Nancy scratched that awfully itchy nose, and whisked herself toward the windows.

The sound alerted Steve immediately. "Hey, Gary, look!" he shouted, pointing up toward the church ceiling, where Nancy was climbing up a long, colorful banner and heading for an open window.

"Let's get out of here!" Gary exclaimed, running toward the back door of the church—and right into the waiting arms of six of the village's finest policemen.

Steve shot his arms up into the air. "I didn't do it! I didn't do it!" he insisted.

Nancy watched as the two thugs were placed in police cars and carted off to jail. She had a great view, since the window she'd climbed out of led directly to the roof of the church. She turned, and waved to the crowd below. "Hi, everybody!" she yelled.

Everyone in the crowd cheered. Well, almost everyone. Carson Drew was too upset at the sight of his daughter perched precariously on the roof of a church to do much more than stare at her.

"Hold on, Nancy," Chief McGinnis called up to her. "We've got the fire department here."

"That's all right, Chief," Nancy assured him. "I'll be down in a jiffy." She reached into her sleuth bag and pulled out a long fishing line. She attached one end to a nearby rain gutter mount and threaded the other end through a mountain-climbing clip. Then she carefully shimmied her way down the side of the church to the ground.

Carson Drew raced to his daughter's side. "Are you okay?" he asked anxiously.

"I'm fine, Dad," Nancy replied. "Really! In the sleuthing business this kind of thing happens all the time. It really isn't a big deal."

"It *is* a big deal!" her father shouted, looking even more upset than he had while she was on the roof. "I ran here from the courthouse in the middle of an eviction case, which the judge . . . He didn't appreciate it."

Nancy looked down at the ground sheepishly. But before she could apologize for making her dad leave in the middle of a trial—not a great move on the part of any attorney—Ned tapped her on the shoulder.

"Is now a better time?" he asked, holding out a small gift box. "Because I wanted to give you this."

Nancy's eyes opened wide at the sight of the box. Before she could reach for the box and open it, though, Chief McGinnis and several of his officers surrounded her, pushing Ned out of the way. A newspaper photographer took several pictures of Nancy and the police, and of Charlie, the security guard, being assisted out of the building, his arms still tied behind his back.

"Well, your hunch was right on the nose, Nancy. I just wish you could have clued us in a little earlier," Chief McGinnis said as the flashbulbs popped.

"Say 'cheese' to all the people!" Bess shouted, snapping a few pictures of her own.

"Nancy, what are we going to do without you?" Pastor Murray asked.

"It's only for a few months," Nancy said, trying to sound upbeat. "I'll be back."

But Nancy wasn't nearly as happy about leaving River Heights as she was trying to sound. In fact, the idea of living in Los Angeles for a few months while her father worked on a big case out there seemed scarier than any mystery she'd ever solved.

Pastor Murray smiled kindly at Nancy. "You're the image of your mother," he told her. "Do you remember her at all?"

Nancy bit her lip, trying to remember anything about her mother. She had died when Nancy was just ten years old. Any memories Nancy had of her at all were really just a blur. "No," Nancy replied sadly.

"She was such a lovely woman," Pastor Murray recalled, "so kind and intelligent."

"Just like you, Nancy," Chief McGinnis chimed in.

At just that moment Carson Drew drove up, sitting behind the wheel of Nancy's blue roadster convertible. From the look on his face Nancy could tell he didn't want to be kept waiting. "Bye, everybody," she said, racing off toward the car.

Ned hurried after her, the small gift box still in his hand, but Nancy was gone before he could get near her.

# CHAPTER 2

The silence in Nancy's car was very uncomfortable. Her dad wasn't the kind of man to yell and scream when he was angry, but sometimes his quiet disapproval could be a lot worse.

"You know, I've been fine with the mystery stuff when it was a stolen bracelet or a missing kitten, but this one . . ." Carson Drew took a deep breath. "Starting now, I want you to spend some time like a normal teenage girl—if such a thing exists."

"Dad . . . ," Nancy protested.

But her father wasn't caving in this time. "I want you to promise. NO MORE SLEUTHING. At least while we're in California," he insisted. "You'll go to school; you'll go shopping. You'll spend some time with teenagers. It's what you're supposed to be doing. Give it a try."

Nancy slumped down in her seat and frowned. The idea of months in California without a mystery definitely did not appeal. She sat there racking her brain for the perfect argument. But nothing came to her.

Nancy's father pulled up in front of their small clapboard house and turned off the car engine. He looked into his daughter's sad eyes and tried to explain why he was moving her away from her home in River Heights. "You know I've always picked cases that help people," he began.

Nancy nodded. "People first," she said, quoting her father.

"That's right," Carson said with a proud smile. "But this one is a little different. If everything goes well, I could start making some real money."

Nancy stared at her father strangely. She'd never heard him speak like this. Money had never been a priority for him. "We have enough money, Dad," she told him.

"I'll be the judge of that, thank you," Carson joked. "At any rate I'm starting something new . . ." He paused for a moment, trying to put his thoughts in order. "I can't be worrying about—"

Before he could finish the sentence, his cell phone rang. No more time for father-daughter chats. This was business. "How are you, John? . . . Yeah, I'll meet you at the deposition as soon as our train gets in. . . . Oh, we don't have an airport out here. . . . I wish I *were* kidding."

As her father walked toward their house, Nancy slumped down even farther in her seat and folded her arms. This trip was sounding worse and worse every minute. And yet, her father seemed so happy about it. She couldn't ruin that for him, even though—

"This is a terrible development!"

Nancy became startled as a voice came from the backseat of her car. She turned around quickly, and came face-to-face with . . . Bess and George. Her two best buds had obviously been hiding back there during the entire ride. They had heard everything.

"What are you going to do?" Bess continued. "You *have* a mystery to solve in La-La Land."

Nancy sighed. It was true. She'd already lined up an amazing case to solve while she was away. Of course her father didn't know a thing about it. And he wasn't going to find out. Not if she could help it.

"I'll figure something out," she told her friends. "I hope," she added quietly as she got out of the car and started up the walk to her house.

○━

The next morning, as Nancy dragged her suitcase onto the porch of her house, she spotted Ned walking toward her. He still had that little box in his hand.

"Ned." She greeted him with a genuine smile. She was so glad he'd come to say good-bye.

Ned smiled back. "With all the commotion I didn't get to give you this."

Nancy's heart was thumping as she took the gift from his hands and gingerly opened the top. "I needed a new compass," she said, looking down at the round silver object in the box. "The old one was wobbly. Thank you."

"See that arrow?" Ned asked, excitedly pointing at the arrow in the center of the silver compass. "It's calibrated so that when you're in Los Angeles . . ." He blushed slightly at the sentiment. "It points the way back to River Heights."

"Oh, Ned," Nancy said quietly. She reached out and hugged him. They stood there for a moment, and then pulled apart, both blushing slightly.

"I just don't know if I'll get to use it," Nancy said with a frustrated shrug.

"Why?"

"Well, my dad let me choose the house we're going to live in, so I chose one with—"

"With a mystery?" Ned asked knowingly.

Nancy nodded. He knew her so well. "But not just any mystery," she explained, her voice gaining excitement at the thought of it. "It's one of the greatest unsolved cases of all times: Dehlia Draycott."

Ned looked at her blankly.

"The movie actress?" Nancy tried. But there was still no recognition on Ned's face. "Before your time," she sighed. Then she pulled out her favorite Pee-Chee folder and opened it to reveal a pile of old newspaper clippings and photos featuring the face and home of a glamorous actress from the 1970s. "Twenty-five years ago, at the height of her fame, she disappeared for five months," Nancy explained. "Nobody knew where. When she came back, she threw a giant party. But she never went downstairs to greet her guests. She was found floating in the pool . . . dead."

"Gee, it sounds like fun," Ned said sarcastically.

But his sarcasm was lost on Nancy. "I know, right?" she asked excitedly. "It really is one of the greatest mysteries of all time! But I didn't tell my dad about the house, and now he won't let me do any sleuthing. I mean, there was a hostage situation at the church, so I can sort of see his point, but—"

Before Nancy could finish her sentence her father stepped out onto the porch. She clammed up immediately. No sense upsetting him right now.

"Hi, Ned," Carson Drew greeted the boy. "Bye, Ned. Gotta scoot, Nancy."

A moment later Hannah Gruen, the housekeeper who

had cared for Nancy and her father ever since Nancy's mother had died, came racing out onto the porch with a tin of fresh baked goodies in her hands. She was followed closely by Bess and George.

"Mr. Drew, here are some pfeffernuss, just in case, and some ginger cupcakes," Hannah said, handing him the tin and fighting back tears. "You'll be hungry on the train."

Hannah wasn't the only one trying not to cry. It was a struggle for George and Bess as well.

"Bye, Nancy," George said, trying not to sniffle too much. "Have a safe train ride, okay? Don't get hurt, and please, you have to keep in contact."

"Bye, Nancy," Bess echoed. "See you soon. I'll miss you. Call me and write us!"

Ned stood there quietly. There was so much to say, and yet he couldn't get any of it out.

"Um, Ned," Nancy said, looking him squarely in the eye. "Don't worry about that guy from *Smallville*. He's not my type." Then she turned and walked bravely toward the taxi that was waiting for them.

As she walked off, Ned smiled to himself. So Nancy *had* heard him at the church the day before. She knew what he was feeling. But as she walked away, something she'd just said hit him. "You have a type?" he called out after her.

But Nancy was already gone.

# CHAPTER 3

It was hard to believe that Los Angeles and River Heights were in the same world, never mind the same country. Nancy had thought she'd seen it all: angry burglars with low blood sugar issues, conniving carnival clowns, soulless swindlers, and other strange people. But nothing in all of her sleuthing had ever prepared her for the cast of characters she saw when she stepped out of the train station in Los Angeles.

There were angry gang members with chains on their low-slung jeans, walking alongside slick businessmen in designer suits and ties, both trying to avoid the sun-drenched teenagers in ratty shorts skateboarding along the sidewalk. And *they* seemed normal compared to some of the other people who lined the streets of Los Angeles.

Nancy was busy staring at all the passersby when a car horn interrupted her thoughts. Her father had secured their rental car, and he pulled up on the side of the road. It was time to go home. Well, to Dehlia Draycott's home, actually, but for the next few months it would be Nancy's as well.

As they drove off toward the Hollywood Hills, Nancy couldn't help but notice how quickly her father had begun to look like the other drivers in Los Angeles. For starters, while Nancy was enjoying the sights—Grauman's Chinese Theatre, the palm trees, the throngs of tourists with their ever-snapping cameras—her father was busy talking to his new office on his cell phone.

As they drove onto a tiny street high up in the hills, Nancy remarked, "Hey, Dad, don't you think people who talk on cell phones miss things?"

"Like what?" he wondered.

"Like that woman in the street—"

*Screech!* The sound of the car tires was deafening as Carson Drew stopped short, narrowly avoiding hitting the woman who'd been crossing the street in front of them.

Surprisingly, the woman wasn't angry at all. In fact, she acted as though almost being mowed over by an oncoming car was the most usual thing in the world. Sh strolled over and tapped on the window. "Mr. Drew?" she asked. "Nancy?"

"Yes?" Mr. Drew asked, clearly surprised that this stranger knew his name.

"Hi," the woman continued. "Thank you so much for not running me over." She held out her perfectly manicured hand. "I'm Barbara Barbara, of Heritage Realty. You're here!" She gestured to the large black iron gates behind her. "I'm gonna get right out of your way," she added, stepping aside so Carson could drive up to the house.

Nancy's eyes opened wide with excitement as the car pulled up past the overgrown green lawn and stopped just before the old frayed awning. It was exactly how she'd imagined it.

Her father, however, felt differently. "It's not really what I had in mind," Carson mentioned to Barbara Barbara as he stepped out of the car and followed the real estate agent inside the house. He glanced at the dust-covered mantel in the living room. "Especially considering the price."

"As I told your daughter on the phone," Barbara Barbara explained, "you pay a premium for mystery—"

quick movement of her hand Nancy knocked coatrack, stopping Barbara before she word. "Oh, I am such an oaf," Nancy apologize, Ms. Barbara. You were saying there's a premium for history, for architectural significance. I mean, Dad, look at this woodwork."

Barbara Barbara looked strangely at Nancy but didn't argue. "Yeah, what she said," she told Mr. Drew, leading them into the salon in the center of the ground floor.

Nancy stared at the giant portrait of Dehlia Draycott, which was hanging above the fireplace. She really had been a magnificent woman, with slick dark hair, and brown eyes that always seemed filled with excitement and daring. Her gaze was inescapable.

"Who's this?" Carson asked Barbara.

"Dehlia Draycott," the real estate agent replied, sounding quite surprised at the question. "The late, great film legend— this was her home! Didn't your daughter tell you?"

Carson looked suspiciously at Nancy. "We've both been somewhat busy," he said. Just then his cell phone began to ring. It was back to business.

As Mr. Drew walked outside to talk to his office, Barbara Barbara headed up the stairs to show Nancy the second floor. She turned for a minute to study the teenager's prim traveling dress and straight golden brown hair. "You know, with a little tweaking you could be adorable."

Nancy wasn't quite sure what to say to that. "Um? Thank you?" she tried.

"Yes, you're a makeover waiting to happen!" Barbara

Barbara continued. "I'm going to give you the name of my stylist." She stopped for a moment and stood completely still. "Did you hear something?" she asked Nancy. "I suddenly got a chill."

Nancy listened for a moment. At first there was nothing but silence. And then, suddenly, a soft wave of noise washed over her, like the gentle sound of someone breathing. The young detective wasn't sure what to make of it. She said nothing, but her sleuth senses were in high gear as she continued following Barbara Barbara on the tour of the house.

"Have a look around if you want," the agent said as they reached the second floor. Barbara Barbara then headed off into one of the bedrooms, checking that everything was in order.

The sight of a figure in the dark hallway stopped Nancy cold. She was certain she saw a woman coming toward her. Well, not a woman, exactly. More like a filmy, transparent image of a woman. If Nancy hadn't known better, she'd have sworn it was a ghost.

The ghost of Dehlia Draycott!

"Don't be afraid," the filmy image cooed, beckoning Nancy to come closer. "Please don't be afraid of me. I'm here to help you. You don't understand, I'm here to help you."

Nancy stood there, riveted by the voice of the woman in the hallway. Nancy's eyes were wide open as she tried to remain calm.

Barbara Barbara, however, didn't seem to be making any attempt at calmness. "Aahhhhhhhhh," she screamed out. Then, a moment later, she began to laugh hysterically. "God, I love that," she joked. "They fall for it every time. That's a projector. It's from one of her movies." She pointed to a small video projector that was mounted on a platform near the ceiling. "There are so many booby traps all over this house. People get so scared sometimes they wet their pants."

"Where's the gift shop?" Nancy asked wryly. How embarrassing—a trained detective like herself being fooled by a movie projector? It was the oldest trick in the book. Or one of them, anyway.

Nancy's sarcasm was lost on Barbara. "That's the spirit," Barbara cheered.

But Nancy's spirits were actually low at the moment. She wasn't looking forward to what she had to say. "Look, Ms. Barbara, I know I called asking for a house with a mystery, but . . . um . . . things have changed and . . . er . . . it's complicated, but we're going to need a different house."

Barbara Barbara smiled. "Oh, honey-cheeks," she

replied in a voice dripping with sugar. "Read the fine print. No refunds. No exchanges. Besides, there's nothing else available in your price range."

Nancy nodded. Despite the disappointed frown that still lingered on her face, there was a bit of excitement racing through her veins. She'd have to stay in the mansion with the mystery. Hey, it wasn't as though she hadn't tried, right?

After a complete tour of the second floor of the house, Nancy and Barbara Barbara headed back downstairs. As they reached the ground floor, Nancy's father emerged from the downstairs bathroom. His face was white as a ghost.

"Something just happened in the bathroom that I am at a loss to explain," he said, trying to remain calm.

"The house has a haunted theme. It's like a theme park," Nancy said quickly, trying to gloss over the whole mystery thing. "It's so fun, right, Dad?

Nancy's father looked at her curiously and then glanced back at the bathroom door. "No," he replied. It was obvious that a haunted theme park was not his idea of home.

Moving on seemed the best way for Nancy to avoid any arguments with her father, so she turned and headed off for a look at the kitchen. But before she could enter the room, she ran smack into a strange man with gray hair and a sour look on his face.

"Oh, did I mention there's a strange caretaker?" Barbara Barbara asked Nancy and Carson, as a way of introducing the fellow. "He lives in an apartment down the hill. I'm sorry, what's your name again?" she asked him.

"Leshing," the caretaker answered in a deep voice. He stared at Nancy peculiarly. "Please let me know if there's anything I can do for you."

Nancy held out her hand. "Nancy Drew." She introduced herself with a smile. "Thank you very much."

Mr. Leshing shook Nancy's hand, but he did not smile back. He just moved slightly to the side, allowing Nancy to enter the kitchen.

As Nancy checked out the fridge, she couldn't help noticing that the vibes she was getting from the old caretaker were far colder than the air coming from the open freezer door.

# CHAPTER 4

By the time night fell, Nancy had almost finished setting up her bedroom. She'd chosen a guest room on the second floor. The room was small, but it was the least fancy of all the bedrooms in the house. Still, there was a shimmery—if dusty—chandelier overhead and ornate carvings in the woodwork.

As she pulled her Pee-Chee folder of Dehlia Draycott clippings and her favorite pair of beaded moccasins from her bag and placed them on the bed, Nancy heard footsteps coming down the hall. She stood and moved toward the hallway. Someone was definitely coming toward her room.

"Dad?" she called out. But there was no response.

"Mr. Leshing?" she tried. But again no one answered. The footsteps stopped.

Nancy shrugged. It was probably just another special effect of some sort, maybe an audio recording from one of Dehlia Draycott's films. Hadn't Barbara Barbara warned her that there were plenty of booby traps in the house?

Nancy walked back into her room to continue unpacking. She reached for her moccasins and her folder, but they were no longer on the bed where she'd left them.

Now *that* was strange. No image from a film projector or voice from a tape recorder could have taken those. Someone had definitely been in her room and stolen her things—in the flesh! There was only one thing to do.

○—

About one hour later Carson Drew found his daughter sitting on the front steps of the mansion with a cordless phone in her hand.

"Someone has stolen my moccasins and an important folder," Nancy explained, looking up at her puzzled dad.

"Mysteries just find you, don't they?" Carson said, shaking his head.

Nancy shrugged. "But I'm letting the professionals handle this one," she assured her father. "I'm on hold with the LAPD."

Carson smiled proudly. "Calling the police to solve a

crime. I like it," he told her, obviously pleased with this change in her behavior.

Nancy glanced down at her watch. "It's been fifty-seven minutes," she noted. "They must be having a busy night."

Carson shrugged and headed back into the house. Nancy followed behind, phone in hand. She plopped down in a living room chair and somehow managed to juggle the phone in one hand and a container of take-out Chinese food in the other. As she ate, she waited . . . and waited . . . and waited for a response from the operator at the police department.

Finally someone got on the line and asked Nancy what the trouble was.

"I'd like to report a theft," Nancy told the operator. "A favorite pair of moccasin slippers and a Pee-Chee folder have been stolen. Please send an officer over immediately."

The laughter coming from the other end of the line was so loud it startled Carson Drew, who had fallen asleep on the couch. He sat up and blinked himself awake.

"Someone must have told a joke over at the precinct." Nancy shrugged, trying to hide her frustration as she hung up the phone.

"Yeah, that's it," Carson said, trying not to hurt Nancy's feelings.

"Because it would be irresponsible for a police

department to laugh at a crime."

"You're right," Carson replied, trying to be agreeable, and then he stood and headed up the stairs for bed.

Nancy followed close behind. But despite the long train trip, and all of her unpacking, she wasn't tired enough to sleep. She lay in bed with her mind racing as the Mystery of the Disappearing Folder and Moccasin Slippers began to form in her mind.

No. *No mysteries*, Nancy reminded herself. She had promised. Finally she turned on the light and pulled an especially dull book—*Advanced Sand-Castle Making*—from the night stand. Surely that would help her fall asleep. But as she began to read, Nancy heard footsteps coming down the hall—the same creaking footsteps she'd heard earlier that evening.

Nancy stayed completely still as she listened for the sound of her father's snoring coming from his room. Sure enough, Carson Drew's unique snore could be heard all the way down the hall. So Nancy got out of bed, picked up the telephone and dialed a number that had been scribbled on a piece of paper.

A moment later a man's deep voice answered. "Hello?"

"Leshing, this is Nancy," she whispered into the phone. "I needed to prove your whereabouts. Go back to sleep."

As she hung up the phone, she was more confused than ever. Someone had been in that hallway earlier. She was sure of it. But if it hadn't been her father or Mr. Leshing, who could it have been?

Well, whoever it was, he was back. Nancy could hear the footsteps in the hallway getting closer and closer. She put on her robe and prepared to go investigate the noise.

And then suddenly Nancy whirled around and came face-to-face with Mr. Leshing!

"Someone's in the house," she whispered to him, trying hard not to appear afraid. She paused for a moment, as a thought suddenly occurred to her. "How did you get here so quickly?" she demanded.

Mr. Leshing's back bristled slightly. "If you're accusing me . . . ," he began.

Nancy ignored him, and instead focused her attention on the creaking noise that was now coming from overhead. "The attic," she whispered, bolting out of her room and heading into the hallway. Leshing followed close behind.

As Nancy hurried up the attic stairs, she noticed something very odd. It sounded as though someone were coming down the stairwell at the very same time. Of course *that* was impossible. Nancy would have passed the person along the way if there had been someone there. When Nancy entered the attic, it was completely empty.

And there were no signs that anyone had been up there.

"How is it possible for someone to be in the attic and then escape while we're coming up the stairs?" Nancy wondered out loud.

Suddenly Nancy's father appeared in the doorway. He was groggy, disheveled, and obviously in need of sleep. "The Four Seasons hotel isn't haunted," he suggested. "What do you say?"

"Dad, you hate hotels," Nancy reminded him.

"Spa treatments," Carson Drew mused. "Room service . . ."

But Nancy was no longer listening to her father. She'd focused her attention on a nearby collection of old boxes—particularly the box that was overflowing with books.

"Those books must have been Dehlia's," she deduced.

"Probably, yes," Mr. Leshing replied.

"May I borrow some?" Nancy asked.

Mr. Leshing frowned. "If it were up to me, I wouldn't let anybody in the house, period," he replied sternly. "But you're paying the rent, so do what you want."

Nancy was surprised by his sudden anger. "I'm sorry," she apologized. "I didn't mean to . . ."

But Leshing was in no mood for apologies. His body language was pure ice as he moved toward the attic door. He turned for a moment, as if to say something, and then stopped himself. "Good night," he murmured, climbing back down the stairwell.

Carson Drew eyed his daughter suspiciously. "So, it turns out there was a mystery here after all."

"Dad, that mystery stuff is so boring to me now. I've completely moved on. It was really just a phase. Like papier-mâché or puppets," Nancy assured him. "Gone . . . forever."

Carson nodded. "Got it." But it was clear from his expression that he didn't believe a word his daughter was saying.

Nancy didn't really believe it either. She wanted to obey her father. She really did. But the mystery of Dehlia's death was too huge an opportunity for her to give up. It was beckoning her—just as the image of Dehlia had done earlier in the day.

Even the *idea* of sleep was impossible now. So Nancy decided to do some reading—real reading. Perhaps the best way to understand what had happened to Dehlia Draycott was to try to understand the kind of person the actress really was. And at the moment the only way Nancy could figure how to do that was to read the books that Dehlia had read, to discover what had interested her.

It was an odd reading list for sure—books with titles such as *The Well of Loneliness*, *The Light in the Darkness*, *Embracing Solitude*, and a Vincent Price cookbook. The cookbook, Nancy noted, had been signed by the horror movie star himself.

From what Nancy could figure, despite the fact that the actress had had millions of fans, and had been surrounded by paparazzi, actors, and movie moguls, Dehlia Draycott had been a lonely woman with a love of scary movies.

As Nancy opened the cover of *The Well of Loneliness*, an old yellowed piece of paper fell onto her lap. After a quick perusal Nancy deduced that it was a letter from Dehlia. It seemed the letter had never been mailed, and Nancy wondered if the actress had intended for the person she'd written it to to ever receive it. Had Dehlia decided not to mail the letter, or had she been killed before she could put it in the mail?

Although the page was filled with cross-outs and revisions, Nancy was able to make out what Dehlia had written on the paper.

Z-
I'm ~~very~~ sorry to have vanished like I did. I know you have been looking for me. ~~I'm~~ Something happened last week. I can't be the Dehlia I was anymore. I am writing a new will. I ~~need~~ need to make provisions for someone else.
-D

Nancy's mind raced as she read the letter again and again. "D is Dehlia," she thought out loud. "But who is Z? And who is this someone else?"

The young detective paused midthought. She had to stop this. *Now.* Her father had been clear. No sleuthing.

But was this really sleuthing? She was only thinking out loud, and reading a book.

"No, you're not sleuthing," she told herself. "You're just reading a letter that happens to be a major clue in a fantastically famous mystery. But that means nothing to you. You're going to go to bed and be reasonable, Nancy. You're going to a new school tomorrow. You're going to make wonderful new friends. You're a normal teenager. You really are."

Still, deep down, Nancy knew she wasn't a normal teenager. And no amount of talking to herself was ever going to change that.

# CHAPTER 5

The crowd of teenagers all watched as the new girl made her way into Hollywood Hills High. It was easy to pick her out. She was the only one in the entire school wearing a dress that went almost down to her knees, or who had a string of pearls around her neck. She wasn't drinking diet soda, or flirting heavily with the boys.

If Nancy noticed everyone looking at her, she didn't seem to mind. Rather, she smiled at everyone she passed, hopeful that someone would smile back. But no one did. They just stared.

And they kept on staring as Nancy sat in on each of her classes. It seemed as though she were the only teen in the entire school who had any idea of what was going on. In algebra class she was the only one who was able to quote the quadratic formula from memory; in gym she was the only one who actually *ran* down the track during the four-hundred-meter race; and in wood shop her scale model of Paris's cathedral of Notre Dame certainly stood out among the crudely formed wooden coat hooks, bookends, and shelves.

But it was in drama class where Nancy made her biggest impression. She stood up in front of the entire class and recited her favorite Shakespearean lines: "O happy dagger! This is thy sheath; there rest, and let me die."

Two incredibly fashionable girls in the front row, Inga and Trish, stared up at her, mesmerized. Even the drama teacher seemed surprised by her performance.

"Th-thank you," she stammered. "But I just wanted your name, dear. Please have a seat."

It was a very long morning. By the time Nancy arrived at the cafeteria, she was hungry—and feeling very lonely. Back in River Heights she would have already been seated at her regular table with Ned, Bess, and George. But here in Hollywood she didn't know a soul. Finally she spotted some familiar faces—the girls from drama class, Inga and Trish. She didn't actually know them, but at least she recognized them. She walked over to their table and sat down.

Inga watched with amazement as Nancy pulled a red-and-white checkered cloth napkin from her brown lunch bag, lay the napkin out like a tablecloth, and then proceeded to unpack her chicken-salad finger sandwiches with the crusts cut off, carrot sticks with herb dipping sauce, a perfectly sliced apple, one of Hannah's flawless white cupcakes, and a thermos of hot cocoa.

As Nancy picked up a sandwich, she noticed a boy staring at her. He looked much younger than the other kids—too young, in fact, to even be in high school.

"Hey, baby," he greeted her. "How you doin'?"

Nancy gave him a nervous smile, and then focused her attention on her sandwich.

Inga looked over at the display of food in front of Nancy, and then at her own tray, which was stocked with french fries, diet cola, and a slice of pizza. She pulled her Sidekick from her pocketbook and began texting like a maniac.

A moment later Inga's message appeared on Trish's Sidekick.

*I'm sitting next 2 Martha Stewart*

Trish laughed and texted back.

*OMG I'm gonna steal that cupcake while U distract*

Inga nodded and plastered a stiff grin onto her face. "Hi," she said to Nancy.

"Hello," Nancy replied, flashing her genuine smile.

"I noticed you were wearing penny loafers," Inga remarked, pointing toward the floor. "Did your podiatrist suggest them, or are you being ironic?"

"I like old-fashioned things," Nancy told her.

Inga quickly surveyed Nancy's lengthy dress, pearls, and loafers. "Oh, we've noticed," she said.

"Penny loafers are practical," Nancy told her.

Inga flashed her another phony grin. "Well, we may be on the brink of a penny loafer fashion moment," she remarked, with just a touch of sarcasm in her voice. Out of the corner of her eye, Inga spotted Trish with the cupcake in hand. "Or not," she added, getting up from her seat and dashing off to another table with Trish, leaving Nancy alone and cupcakeless.

A few moments later Inga and Trish were happily splitting their newly stolen cupcake when the same freshman boy who had greeted Nancy earlier plopped down at the table beside them.

"Can't you get your stupid little brother to leave us alone?" Trish begged Inga.

Inga glared at her younger brother, Corky, demanding that he leave. But Corky didn't budge.

"I saw that, you dirty cupcake thieves," he barked at his sister and her friend. "Give it back."

Inga shoved a small piece of the cupcake into his hand. "Shut up," she ordered.

Corky popped the dessert into his mouth, and sighed. "That's a good cupcake," he murmured.

"It's the most delicious thing I've tasted since . . ." Inga thought for a moment. "Midnightish, last Saturday."

Trish giggled. Inga and Corky joined in.

From across the room Nancy watched the three of them enjoying her cupcake and laughing at her expense. But instead of getting angry she felt sorry for them. Obviously they were enjoying her homemade cupcake because all of the foods served in the cafeteria were unhealthy. This cupcake was made with only the finest fresh ingredients— that was all Hannah ever used.

Nancy was determined to help her new classmates as best she could. She packed up her lunch and immediately made her way to the principal's office. A moment later she was making her feelings known.

"I feel strongly that students should be given more nutritious alternatives in the cafeteria," Nancy told the principal. "Perhaps a salad bar."

The principal nodded woodenly. "A salad bar. Terrific idea."

"Let me see," Nancy remarked, trying to remember some of the other things she wanted to alert him of. "Oh, yes. I believe there may be traces of lead paint in the utility shed next to the volleyball courts."

"Lead paint is bad, right?" the principal asked.

"Very bad," Nancy confirmed.

As Nancy continued her dialogue with the principal, she was unaware that Trish and Inga were right outside the office, listening in on the conversation. For some reason they were positively fascinated by Nancy.

"She keeps finding fresh and exciting ways to be a freak," Inga whispered to Trish.

"And finally," Nancy continued, "I urge you to offer a course in CPR. I noticed it wasn't part of the curriculum. I'm certified and I have found great peace of mind in knowing I may save a life some day."

Inga and Trish exchanged looks. Amazing. They'd never seen anything like this girl. Nobody at Hollywood Hills High ever had.

Hollywood Hills High School may have been different from her school back in River Heights, but there was one thing both schools had in common—a great basketball team. As Nancy sat down in the bleachers to watch that afternoon's game, she breathed a sigh of relief. No matter how different one high school might be from another, all high school gyms looked pretty much the same. They all had bleachers, basketball hoops, and scoreboards, and they all smelled of sweaty gym socks. For the first time all day Nancy felt at home.

But Nancy's peaceful viewing of the game did not last long. Suddenly she heard screams coming from the doorway. She looked over to see Inga and Trish screaming at the tops of their lungs. That strange boy from the cafeteria was lying on the floor, his arms and legs flailing.

"Corky! Corky!" Trish screamed.

"Oh my god! My brother's choking!" Inga added frantically. "No! Please, does anyone know CPR? Does anyone know CPR?"

Nancy rose up calmly and began climbing down the bleachers and over to the doorway. "I do!" she called back to Inga. "I know CPR."

As soon as she reached Corky, Nancy dropped to her knees and, completely ignoring the crowd that had gathered around her, expertly surveyed the boy's condition. The boy was holding a pretzel with a bite taken out of it. It was possible that that was what he was choking on. "Don't worry, everything's going to be fine," she told Corky in a soft, soothing voice as she opened his mouth and deftly stuck her fingers inside to check for an obstruction.

Suddenly Corky took a turn for the worse. His eyes rolled back in his head and his body went limp.

"Oh my god," Inga cried out again.

Nancy grabbed Corky from behind and pushed heavily up under his rib cage. A huge piece of unchewed pretzel flew out of his mouth—hurtling straight toward Inga and Trish. They leaped out of the way of the flying mass of mushed-up dough.

Despite the fact that his airway was now free, Corky still did not appear to be breathing. But Nancy did not panic. Instead she laid him back down, placed some rolled-up sweat pants under his neck, and prepared to give him mouth-to-mouth resuscitation. But before she could place her mouth on his, Corky opened his eyes and wrapped his arms around Nancy's body.

"I didn't think it was possible," Corky told her loudly, "but you're even more attractive close up."

"You idiot!" Inga scolded her younger brother. "You were supposed to kiss her. Lip-lock! That was the plan!"

Nancy's head began to spin. Through a haze of humiliation, she could hear everyone in the gym laughing at her. She was mortified. In her entire life no one had ever treated her this way. Slowly she stood and waded her way through the sea of laughing high school students and out of the building. There didn't seem to be anything else to do.

projector. A small window had been cut into the wall of the crawl space, just big enough to allow the projector's image to shine through. The angle of the projector allowed the film to be projected right onto the living room wall. Beside the film projector were stacks of giant film reels—the old-fashioned kind they used to use in movie theaters.

Nancy glanced at the titles on the film canisters. These were all rough cuts of old Dehlia Draycott movies. Not the actual finished films but the daily pieces of film that had been shot—canisters of individual scenes, some shot over and over again until the director and actors were satisfied. Watching dailies was not the best way to catch a movie, but it was definitely a good way to search for clues.

After replacing a few bulbs and feeding the delicate film through the old-fashioned machine, Nancy was ready for her late-night movie marathon. She curled up on the couch and watched as Dehlia Draycott hit her mark.

"Action!" the director shouted from off-camera.

Dehlia's beautiful face came into view. She was wearing an ankle-length velvet dress and walking across a movie set with a handsome actor.

"I'm looking forward to the journey, and I'm . . ." The actress stopped for a minute and looked helplessly off to the side. "What's the line? Sorry."

"Cut!" the director shouted. And someone read the next line to Dehlia. A moment later the director once again shouted "Action." Dehlia began her lines again.

"I'm looking forward to the journey, and I don't care that a woman traveling unaccompanied is considered shameful," she declared in her engaging voice. "I've done nothing wrong. My heart is . . ." Dehlia stopped again and frowned. Then, looking off-camera at someone—probably the director—she said, "I'll get it. It's okay."

Nancy watched the screen, fascinated, as Dehlia got ready for her third take of the scene. Something was different about the actress this time. Her face seemed more ashen, and her eyes were unfocused, as though something wasn't right with her. And yet she tried the scene again.

"I'm looking forward to the journey, and I don't care that a woman traveling alone . . . that . . . she . . ." Dehlia stopped suddenly. "I . . . feel sick . . . I need to stop."

Nancy was on the edge of her seat. The real-life drama on the screen was more fascinating than any movie script could be. She was so entranced with what was happening on the screen in front of her that she didn't notice that someone else had entered the room. Then, suddenly, she felt a familiar presence.

Nancy turned around quickly and came face-to-face with Mr. Leshing. He was standing behind her, watching. And he looked furious.

"What're you doing?" he demanded. "This is not for guests!"

"I'm sorry," Nancy apologized, jumping up from the couch. "The door was unlocked."

But Leshing wasn't listening to her anymore. He'd already made his way into the small projector room. Nancy followed him in and began to switch off the projector. But Mr. Leshing stopped her. "No, leave it on," he said, his eyes following the film as it spun from one reel of the projector to the next. "There was a time when you couldn't just pop a disc into a box. You had to run actual film in front of a light." He looked around and sighed. "I haven't been in here since the night she—" He stopped, realizing he had said too much.

But Nancy wasn't about to let something like that drop. "You were here the night she died?" she asked. "How long did you work for her?"

"The year I got out of the service I went to work at the studio," Mr. Leshing explained. "They sent me over here to project a movie for her. She asked me to stay and take care of her, so I did. That was in 1971."

Nancy nodded slowly, absorbing the information. "When she disappeared, did you know where she went?" she asked.

"No."

The tone in Mr. Leshing's voice made it clear that he didn't want to answer any more questions. But Nancy couldn't stop. There was so much she wanted—*needed*—to find out.

"She never married," Nancy continued. "And it seems she was very private. But there must have been a man. Someone she loved."

"Every man who met her fell in love with her," Mr. Leshing said. "It couldn't be helped. But I don't know if she ever felt love herself."

Nancy watched the old man for a while, trying to decipher just what it was he had felt for his former employer. But he was a tough read. And after a few seconds Mr. Leshing realized Nancy was staring at him. He turned and left the house, leaving Nancy alone with the celluloid images of Dehlia Draycott.

By the end of the week Nancy had watched hours of dailies and had read everything she could find on the Internet about Dehlia Draycott. And still the actress was as much of a mystery to her as she'd been before. All Nancy had to show for her week of late-night research sessions were circles under her eyes and a bad case of exhaustion. She was really relieved that it was Saturday. Nancy was too tired to make it through one more day of school. Not to mention the fact that she was perfectly happy not to have to face Inga, Trish, or Corky for two days either.

Or so she thought.

Not long after breakfast the doorbell rang. When Nancy opened the front door, she discovered Corky standing there. He smiled apologetically at her.

"Look, I'm sorry about the weirdness the other day," he told Nancy.

"I have to say my feelings were a little bruised," Nancy admitted. She stopped and shot him a brighter smile. "But thank you, Corky. An apology is the sign of a gentleman."

Corky relaxed at the sight of her smile. "Inga roped me into the shenanigans," he told Nancy. "She's my sister, but I think she also might be the devil. Plus, I thought if you gave me mouth-to-mouth, it would be a fantastic way for us to get to know each other. The truth is, you're insane."

Nancy looked at him oddly. This was the strangest apology she'd ever received.

"In, like, an awesome way," Corky assured her. "You're awesome." He blushed slightly and shifted his weight back and forth. "By the way, did you know there was a mystery to this house?" he asked, trying to change the subject.

"Yes, I know," Nancy said with a grin. She turned and

motioned for Corky to follow her inside. "I only recently discovered that movies aren't shot from beginning to end," she explained, leading him up to the attic, which she had been using as her detective workshop for the past week. It was the one place her father was certain not to go.

Corky looked at the photocopied pictures of movie frames that lined the floor of the attic. They were lined up in perfect order.

"I took the last movie Dehlia ever made and reassembled the shots in the order they were photographed," Nancy explained, pointing at a series of photos that had been pinned to the wall. In each photo Dehlia was markedly hiding her stomach—behind a screen, behind a hedge, behind a pillow. Nancy stopped suddenly. "Maybe she was pregnant!" she shouted excitedly.

Corky shook his head. "She didn't have any kids," he told Nancy. "Never married and no kids."

Still, Nancy wasn't convinced. "It's just a hunch," she mused, grabbing a magazine from her pile of research material. "Also, the photograph in this magazine is dated just after her reappearance."

Corky looked at the picture. It didn't seem particularly interesting, just a shot of Dehlia wearing a bathrobe.

But the picture was *extremely* curious as far as Nancy was concerned. "There's an *X* on her robe," she pointed out. "I believe this insignia will tell us where she was hiding during her absence. I checked all the hospitals and hotels that include the letter $X$ but found nothing. I need to find someone who's an expert in clothing. And one more thing," she continued. "There's often a man with her, but he's always obscured: a hand on the edge of the picture, a silhouette or a blur. I think Dehlia called him Z. I have to find out who this man is. And if there's a child out there who doesn't know about his or her mother . . . I just have to solve this!"

Corky had been staring at Nancy with a combination of awe and curiosity. But she'd been so caught up in her own thoughts, she hadn't noticed. Now she finally turned to him. "So what do you think?" she asked.

Corky sighed and flashed a smile. "I think the ability to sleuth is an attractive quality in a woman."

Nancy stared at him for a moment, confused. Then suddenly the attic door slammed shut. She and Corky jumped with fright as a sudden gust of wind scattered the pictures and papers on the floor. Nancy looked curiously around the room. That sudden wind had not been a coincidence. And it hadn't been a ghost, either. Someone had been listening in.

But who?

# CHAPTER 7

Even a teen detective had to eat sometime, so Nancy gratefully accepted Corky's invitation to head to Los Angeles's Union Station for a tasty churro and a look at the city. The churro was delicious, but nothing fed Nancy's appetite for mystery like the movie that was filming near the restaurant where she and Corky had been eating. The actors were wearing outfits that dated back to the 1950s.

"Hey, don't they have a costume department on the set of every film?" she asked Corky.

"Yeah," Corky replied. "But you should know that movie people are kind of crazy."

Nancy wasn't going to let a little craziness stop her from getting the information she needed. A costumer would be the perfect person to ask about how a pregnant woman might be outfitted to disguise her bulging belly. And Nancy was still convinced that Dehlia must have been pregnant when she'd shot those scenes.

Nancy turned and strutted determinedly toward the costume trailer. She stood there for a moment, watching as the film's costumer checked each of the extras who had been outfitted for the film. The costumer walked through the crowd of actors, putting the finishing touches on their leather jackets, pedal pushers, poodle skirts, and slicked-back hair, one by one. The costumer stopped in front of Nancy and examined her rolled up jeans, penny loafers, and peacoat. To her, Nancy looked like the perfect 1950s teen. "You're fine," the costumer told her.

"No, I have a question," Nancy corrected her.

"And I'm out of answers," the costumer retorted. "You look fifties. Go to the set."

"But I was just wondering—" Nancy continued.

"Now!" the costumer insisted.

Just then an assistant began moving through the throng of movie extras. "Okay, we're moving! We're moving, people, we're on our way. Let's go! We are moving!"

The tide of extras shifted onto the set, carrying Nancy along with them. The next thing she knew, the teen sleuth was on the set of a genuine Hollywood movie.

"All right," the director shouted, making his way onto the set and surveying the group of extras that were gathered around the classic cars. "We're going to just shoot the rehearsal." He looked around the area. "Has anyone seen Mr. Fancy-Pants?" he asked angrily.

An actor in a long tan trench coat arrived on the set. "I'm right here, you idiot!" he barked to the director.

The director looked nervously at the extras. "A nickname," he told them, referring to the word "idiot." "I love a nickname."

"It's not a nickname, Andy," the actor insisted. "You really are an idiot."

The director rolled his eyes and began to explain the actor's motivation to him. "All right, you hate crime," he said. "And action!"

The cameras rolled as two actors dressed in police uniforms grabbed an actor playing a criminal. They slapped a pair of handcuffs onto him. Then the star of the film sauntered over.

"Hold him right there, boys," he said, pretending to sneer. "Spider Weintraub, as I live and breathe, you have the right to remain silent. You have the right to an attorney—"

"Excuse me," Nancy interrupted, stepping into the middle of the shot. "I'm sorry. This just feels inauthentic."

"Feels what?" the movie actor demanded. He seemed shocked that a mere extra would interrupt his shot.

"Well, this scene takes place in the fifties, but you're reading the Miranda warning to the suspect," Nancy explained.

The director pushed past the cameramen, cars, and extras and stood in front of Nancy. "Um, excuse me," he demanded, looking around. "Why, in the name of sweet Christmas, is this tiny person talking?"

If Nancy noticed his anger, she certainly didn't show it. "The reading of the Miranda rights upon arrest wasn't the law until 1966," she explained confidently.

The lead actor looked at Nancy with genuine fascination. "Is that right?" he asked her. "What's your name?"

"Nancy Drew."

"Hi," the actor said, holding out his hand. "I'm Bruce."

"All right!" the angry director scolded. "I'll tell you what. Why don't *you* direct the movie, Nancy Drew?" And with that he stormed off the set.

Bruce smiled triumphantly. "Listen, Nancy. Would you consider directing this film? 'Cause we can get rid of this guy in a second."

But Nancy's directing debut would have to wait. A few moments later she was being escorted off the set, at the insistence of the real director. "Is there a law against common courtesy in Los Angeles?" she asked Corky as they walked away.

"Courtesy is so awesome," Corky told her in a voice filled with worship. "I'm really into it."

"In my book, courtesy counts," Nancy said.

Corky stopped and looked her in the eye. "I'd like to read that book, Nancy," he said dramatically.

Just then a giant light from the movie set flashed. The light cast a sharp shadow on the street in the form of a giant X. The figure reminded Nancy of something she'd seen before. As she looked up to see what was casting the shadow, she realized something. That hadn't been an X on Dehlia Draycott's robe at all. "They're palm trees!" she shouted excitedly.

"Okay. What does that mean?" Corky called after her.

"The insignia on her robe," Nancy told him. "It's um . . . something Palms."

"Okay, now I get it," Corky replied. "Just kidding."

○—

Nancy's logic may have been lost on Corky, but the young detective was positive she'd found an important clue. After an extensive Internet search she finally found a California hotel whose logo was two intertwined palm trees forming an X—the Twin Palms resort, located a short drive away in the California desert.

The only way to get to the hotel was to drive there. And with her roadster back in River Heights, Nancy had no choice but to borrow her father's car. She would just have to get the car back to the house before he got home.

The Twin Palms resort was not hard to find. But the information Nancy was looking for proved to be more elusive. Acting on her hunch that Dehlia had in fact been pregnant, Nancy calculated the approximate time that Dehlia had given birth. The photograph of Dehlia in the hotel robe was dated just after her reappearance, and her letter to Z, (in which she said that she was "sorry to have vanished" and that "something that happened last week"), seemed to have been sent around that same time. So Nancy concluded that Dehlia had given birth in a hospital near the Twin Palms resort the week before her reappearance. Unfortunately, the hotel manager was no help to her at all.

"There was a fire some twenty years ago and all the records were burned," he explained to her. "On top of that, I'm afraid our guest list is confidential."

Nancy nodded. She understood all about rules. She was breaking a big one just by being there. But she couldn't stop now. Someone had to be able to tell her if Dehlia Draycott had been pregnant, and if she'd given birth near the resort. Since most babies were born in hospitals, she decided that should be her next stop.

But it seemed the clerk in the hospital's record department wasn't going to be any more help to Nancy than the hotel manager had been.

"You want to know all the children born in one week twenty-four years ago?" he asked her incredulously.

"Well, just the ones given up for adoption," Nancy told him. "See, the birth mother, she may have left money to the child."

"I'm sorry, but those records are sealed. Only a court order can open those records. And even then only by a child seeking a parent." He paused for a moment, studying her face. "Are you the child?"

"No," Nancy replied dejectedly. Then, suddenly her face brightened as an idea came to her. She reached into her sleuth bag and pulled out a small piece of white cake. "Here's a blondie for your trouble," she told the clerk.

Nancy walked away slowly. She knew the clerk would never be able to resist the piece of cake she'd just given him. And once he'd had a bite . . .

"Did you make this?" the clerk called after her.

Nancy stopped and turned around. "No, our housekeeper, Hannah, back in River Heights did. She sent over a tin. She's a wonderful baker."

"It's so weird," the clerk said, taking a bite. "My mother

made these when I was a kid. I haven't had one in years." He took another nibble. "It's perfectly moist."

Nancy grinned. She could tell he was weakening.

"The county recommends a pediatrician to new adoptive parents," the clerk told her finally. "The doctors' files aren't sealed." He wrote a name on a slip of paper that he handed to Nancy. "This might help," he told her.

"Thank you!" Nancy exclaimed.

"You didn't get it from me," he warned.

Nancy nodded in agreement as she left.

The clerk's note took Nancy to an old medical office not far from the hospital. The nurse there was happy to help Nancy. Unfortunately, it seemed she was too disorganized to be of much help.

"Here it is," the nurse said, pulling a folder from her bulging file cabinet. "There were two newborns that week." She looked again. "No, make that three. But, uh, oh, I don't think I can release . . . Let me call headquarters." Just then the phone rang. "Hello? Jimmy?"

As the nurse continued with her phone call, Nancy craned her neck so she could get a look at the folder. Quickly she scribbled down the names that were written on the paper.

By the time the nurse had finished her call, the girl detective was gone.

# CHAPTER 8

Nancy had the names of the three babies who had passed through the medical office that week twenty-four years ago, but finding the one who was Dehlia's child wasn't going to be easy. It seemed there were at least a hundred Martine Dahlbergs, Jane Brightons, and Susan Thabits in the phone book. Still, Nancy planned to meet each and every one of them in the hopes of finding Dehlia's rightful heir.

Nancy drove all around the Los Angeles area knocking on doors, searching for someone who had Dehlia's eyes, or smile, or some other mark that would identify her. But no one seemed to fit the profile until she knocked on the door of a small, dingy apartment in north Hollywood.

A young woman with pretty brown hair came to the door and eyed Nancy suspiciously.

"Is there a Jane Brighton here?" Nancy asked her.

"Depends on who's asking," the brunette replied.

"Were you adopted?" Nancy wondered.

The woman stopped for a moment. "Yeah," she said. "Who are you?"

Nancy was about to respond when a three-year-old girl came running out of the bedroom and hugged her mother. Nancy stared at her in amazement. The child had dark brown hair, huge eyes, and the same high cheekbones as her grandmother. This was Dehlia's granddaughter—which would make the brunette at the door Dehlia's daughter.

"You're who I'm looking for," Nancy told Jane Brighton.

"I am?" Jane asked nervously.

"Hi," Nancy said with a smile designed to put Jane at ease. It worked, and a moment later Nancy was inside the small apartment. It was shabby but neat, and Nancy could tell that Jane was a good mother.

The young sleuth quickly explained why she had come looking for Jane. It was obvious that Jane wanted to believe her, but she definitely had her doubts. Not that Nancy blamed her. It wasn't every day someone discovered her birth mother was a famous movie star who had died mysteriously.

"Did your parents tell you that you were adopted?" Nancy asked Jane.

"It wasn't hard to figure out," Jane replied. "I didn't look anything like them. My mother passed away and then my father—" She looked over at her daughter, Allie, who was happily playing with some toys on the floor. Then she chose her words carefully. "I had to get away from him. I left home early." She paused for a moment, considering the enormity of what she had just learned. "Dehlia Draycott. Wow. I always dreamed that my real mother and father would show up and fix everything that had gone wrong." Tears began to form in her eyes.

"I don't know who your father is," Nancy told her, "but Dehlia may have made a provision for you. And if we can prove you're the daughter, then maybe there's some money."

Jane eyed Nancy suspiciously. "Is this some kind of practical joke?"

"Oh, no," Nancy insisted, shaking her head. "I don't joke."

○━

Nancy had been busy sleuthing for a week now, and somehow she'd managed to keep it all from her father. But

Welcome to

# Los Angeles

We arrived at the house we rented, the Dehlia Draycott Mansion, and it was perfect! It looked exactly as I'd imagined it would!

Our real-estate agent told me that there were booby traps all over the house. I thought the projection of Dehlia was actually her ghost—I can't believe I was so easily fooled!

I heard footsteps in the hallway so I went to investigate.

When I returned, my Pee-Chee folder and moccasins were missing! First I thought it was Leshing, but it wasn't.

In the attic I found a whole box of Dehlia's things—including this letter that she wrote to someone named "Z". . . .

People in L.A. are very different from my friends back home. Like Inga and Trish—they dress like rock stars and have their own Sidekicks. And they think *I*'m nuts!

Even though I told my father I wouldn't sleuth, I just couldn't stop myself from wanting to find out what Dehlia had been like when she was alive.

After watching her dailies I was certain that Dehlia had been pregnant and had given birth to a child before she was killed. Then I realized that the X on her robe was actually two palm trees—an insignia from the hotel she hid out in before she gave birth!

A clue!

With the help of a hospital clerk and a secretary in a doctor's office, I discovered three possible names for Dehlia's daughter.

I knew Jane Brighton was Dehlia's daughter the moment I saw her. I told her everything I knew, but about a week later she and her daughter, Allie, were evicted from their apartment!

I started getting scary phone calls from men telling me to stop investigating the mystery. Someone even tried to run Corky and me over! That meant that I was onto something!

This is the secret passageway that Leshing and the intruders must have used. . . .

Ned was here for my birthday, which was great! The next day I realized that Dehlia had used a line from one of her movies as a clue to where she hid her will in real life. I followed the clue and found her will!

The will!

It turns out that "Z" was Dehlia's lawyer, and he was also the one who murdered her. Leshing is actually Jane's father—he and Dehlia were in love! Another case solved—"Z" was arrested; Jane, Allie, and Leshing met at last; and Dad and I went back to River Heights where we belong. Oh, and I got to see Ned again!

that was proving more and more difficult. Nancy hated lying to her father—she really did. But she just couldn't give up on this mystery now. Not when it could mean so much to Jane and Allie.

So she chose her words very carefully as she sat at the breakfast table with her father before school one morning.

"So, how are you getting on with the kids at school here?" Carson asked.

"They . . . ," Nancy began slowly. "They make me appreciate the kids back in River Heights."

Carson chuckled. "Very diplomatic of you."

"I did make two friends," Nancy continued. "Jane and Allie."

"What class are they in?"

Nancy thought for a minute. "It's kind of . . . history," she told him. She was very relieved when she heard the telephone ring. It was a welcome reprieve from her father's questions. "Hello?" she said.

"Do not look into this matter," the caller threatened in a thick Russian accent. "This Dehlia Draycott business. If you proceed . . . you will be harmed. Do you understand?"

Nancy glanced over at her father, who was now busy reading over some paperwork from the office. "Um, we're not interested in mud–slide insurance," she told the caller. "But thank you for calling. Have a nice day!"

○──

The caller's odd voice and strong warning stayed with Nancy all day as she sat through her classes. And by the end of the day she was exhausted from the effort it took to keep her mind on her lessons instead of the mystery. So she was extremely glad when the final bell rang and she could walk home from school and finally devote her thoughts entirely to Dehlia.

Although Nancy had wanted to be alone to think, Corky wasn't giving her the opportunity. He insisted on walking her home, talking her ear off the whole way.

"I'm twelve, but I skipped a few grades," he told Nancy, explaining what he was doing in high school.

"Because you were ahead academically?" Nancy asked him.

"Heck no," Corky replied. "There just wasn't any action in junior high, so my dad made a few calls. Anyway, I was wondering if we could do, like, a dinner thing? Like Saturdayish? Not a date," he added quickly.

Nancy smiled, and tried to let him down easily. "Corky, you've been really nice to me, but—"

"I'll show you the sights," Corky said quickly. "We'll have a few laughs."

"There's a guy back in River Heights," Nancy explained, reaching into her pocket and fingering the silver compass Ned had given her.

"Oh," Corky replied with a frown. "Okay. But you still have to eat. And it's not a date."

"Okay." Nancy relented. "Seeing as how it's not a— OH MY GOD!"

Nancy gasped and then yanked Corky over to the side of the road, just in time to avoid being hit by an oncoming SUV that had spun out of control. Quickly Nancy grabbed a piece of chain-link fence and heaved it in the direction of the oncoming car. The SUV slammed into the fence, stopped, skidded into reverse, and then started forward again—heading right for Nancy and Corky.

Nancy pushed Corky, sending him up a nearby hill. "Climb up!" she ordered. "Go! Go! Go!"

"That car!" Corky cried out. "It almost hit us!"

And it was still aiming to do just that. Nancy pushed harder on Corky's back, forcing him up the hill as she climbed behind him. She looked down just in time to see the SUV slam into the cement barrier right beneath them. She picked up the pace, which allowed them to escape from the SUV just in time.

It took a few minutes for the two friends to catch their breath and take in what had happened. "I wonder who tried to kill us," Nancy said finally.

"Yeah, I'm wondering that too," Corky agreed. "In fact, I'm kind of freaking out about it."

But Nancy wasn't freaking out. On the contrary, she was actually encouraged by what had just happened. "Usually if someone's trying to kill me it's because I'm on to something." She stopped and looked down at Corky's arm. "Oh, you have a scratch," she said, opening her sleuth kit and pulling out some first aid cream and a Band-Aid. "There were dealer plates on the SUV," she continued, tending to Corky's injury. "I made note of the make, year, and model. Plus, the damage sustained from hitting that barrier could help identify it too."

Corky was amazed. "You're not like the other girls, Nancy," he said, stating the obvious.

○━

The near-death experience with the car only served to pique Nancy's curiosity further, and she desperately wanted to help Jane and Allie. So her next sleuthing stop was at the office of a famous entertainment lawyer named Dashiel Biedermeyer. He had been Dehlia's attorney when she was alive.

Mr. Biedermeyer was a very busy man and not likely to notice a teenager, unless of course he happened to bump into her somewhere—which explained why Nancy was waiting near the entrance to his law firm when he walked outside on his way to a meeting the following afternoon. It was her way of making sure that he bumped into her right away.

"I apologize, sir. Allow me to introduce myself," Nancy said, stepping out in front of him. "My name is Nancy Drew." She reached out her hand and gave him a firm shake. "It's very nice to make your acquaintance."

"'Apologize'? 'Sir'? 'Acquaintance'?" Mr. Biedermeyer repeated. "Could I pay you to teach some manners to my grandchildren and their friends?"

"I'm not sure if I . . . ," Nancy began.

Mr. Biedermeyer looked around at the group of lawyers who had followed him out of his office. "Posture! Eye contact!" he said, praising Nancy's behavior. "Pay attention, people! That's breeding!"

"I was wondering if I could have five minutes to discuss something with you," Nancy asked.

"Anytime at all," he told Nancy. "Here's my card." He waved his hand. In a flash, every one of the lawyers around him whipped out a business card giving the name and address of the law firm.

Right then seemed as good a time as any to Nancy. "Thank you," she said. "It's about one of your clients, a movie star—"

"All of my clients are movie stars, muffin," Mr. Biedermeyer informed her.

Nancy nodded. "I believe I may have found some evidence suggesting—"

But before Nancy could finish the statement, Mr. Biedermeyer's attention had been taken away by someone calling on his cell phone. "I'm very disappointed, Senator," the lawyer said into his cell. "Well, as you know, you do owe me a favor or two. Talk to someone else on your staff. Maybe they can help you with this."

As Mr. Biedermeyer walked off, Nancy stared at the business card in her hand. Maybe this visit hadn't been completely in vain. Quickly she dashed over to Jane's apartment.

○━

Nancy knocked and knocked on the door, but no one answered. Still, she was certain she had heard the sound of a television inside. "Jane? Are you there?" Nancy called out.

Finally the door opened—just a crack. Jane peeked out.

"Hi," Nancy said. "I saw the lawyers who represent the estate today, and they told me—"

"It's all right," Jane said, refusing to open the door any farther. "I don't want any help."

"What do you mean?" Nancy asked. "Don't you want to know if you're Dehlia's daughter?"

Jane began to cry. "Please just leave me alone," she pleaded. "You seem like a nice person. I'm sorry." And with that she closed the door.

Nancy stood there for a moment, pondering what had just happened. Someone had gotten to Jane. That she knew for certain. What she didn't know was who. Or why.

# CHAPTER 9

"The will is in the Chinese box."

Nancy was startled suddenly at the sound of someone's voice inside her room late on Friday night. She opened her eyes and stared directly into the face of Dehlia Draycott!

And then she was gone. Just as suddenly as she had come.

A dream. It had all been a dream.

Or had it? Nancy was pretty sure someone had tapped on her shoulder to wake her up. But now there was no one there. And the only sound in the room was the sound track of an old Dehlia Draycott movie Nancy had been watching when she'd nodded off to sleep. Nancy flicked her DVD player off, and then scribbled a note onto the pad beside her bed.

*The will is in the Chinese box.*

That message was still on Nancy's mind when she woke up the following morning. She leaped out of bed, readied her sleuth kit, and prepared to figure out whether or not there was a Chinese box that could help her solve the mystery of Dehlia Draycott's death.

Her first step was to figure out just what Dehlia could have meant by a Chinese box. To do that, Nancy decided to speak to Mr. Leshing. As Dehlia's caretaker for so many years, he'd surely know what she'd been talking about.

"Miss Draycott collected chinoiserie," Mr. Leshing explained. "Last year the owner sold off the most valuable pieces. Against my wishes."

"Do you remember the name of the dealer?" Nancy asked him.

"You ask a lot of questions," the old caretaker grumbled.

Nancy held up the yellow pages book and opened it to the page for dealers. A name had been circled: K. G. Louie.

"Is this the place?" she asked Mr. Leshing. "I noticed the ad was circled."

"Let me tell you something, young lady," Mr. Leshing replied angrily. "Everyone who has ever tried to piece this all together has run into trouble."

Before Nancy could ask Mr. Leshing just what kind of trouble he was referring to, the phone rang. And as Nancy hurried to pick it up, the old caretaker disappeared.

"Hello?" Nancy said into the receiver.

"So," her father replied, launching into the conversation without even a second for a hello. "You should be getting an early birthday-present-slash-reward thing for going along with my whole no-sleuthing-while-in-California thing."

A pang of guilt hit Nancy hard. "Oh, Dad," she told him. "You shouldn't have. I don't really deserve it." Nancy bit her lip. That was an understatement.

"Yes, you do," her father insisted. "I know it hasn't been easy for you. This'll help me feel a little less guilty."

Just then the doorbell rang. Nancy raced down the stairs with her portable phone in hand.

"But what is it?" Nancy asked, suddenly curious about the reward.

"Just walk outside," her dad told her.

Nancy opened the door and looked out. There was Corky, with a sleek new sports car behind him. Trish was in the driver's seat of the car, with Inga beside her.

"Hi, Corky," Nancy said, now more confused than ever.

"Hi," Corky replied. "My sister dropped me off and

now she won't go away." He turned toward the sports car. "Leave!" he shouted to Inga. But the two girls just sat there in the car, enjoying the show.

And then Nancy spotted her *real* reward. "My roadster!" she shouted into the phone to her father. "How did you get it here?"

Before Carson could answer, Nancy's *other* surprise popped up from his hiding place behind the wheel of the car.

"Happy almost-your-birthday!" Ned shouted.

Nancy ran over and gave Ned a gigantic hug. "You drove this all the way here?" she asked him.

"Uh, yeah," Ned replied with a teasing grin. "It wouldn't fit in my suitcase."

"I've missed this car so much," Nancy said, gently running her hand along the hood of the car. "And you," she assured Ned, noticing the sudden drop in his expression. "I've missed both the car *and* you." She paused for a minute, and glanced over at Corky. "Oh," she said apologetically. "Ned, Corky. Corky, Ned. Ned is my . . . really good friend from back in River Heights."

If Ned had looked slightly dejected before, he seemed downright deflated now. And that wasn't lost on Corky. "River Heights, right," Corky said, trying to sound as sophisticated as he could. "That's in one of those flyover states."

Ned looked from Nancy to Corky and back again. "Did I interrupt something?" he asked Nancy.

"Yes, you did, as a matter of fact," Corky replied, moving closer to Nancy.

Suddenly Nancy heard a deep voice calling her name. It was her dad, still on the phone, waiting for Nancy to remember him.

"Oh, Dad!" she exclaimed happily. "Thank you so much."

Nancy hung up quickly with her father, and then led Ned and Corky into her blue roadster. She wouldn't have minded some alone time with Ned, but she'd already made plans with Corky and she couldn't go back on her word. Still, she was anxious to show Ned around the city—and she had one special place in mind to start with. Chinatown. After all, even with all of these wonderful surprises, Nancy still had a mystery to solve.

As Nancy and the boys drove off, Inga and Trish looked at each other with amazement.

"Corky's going on a date with her?" Inga asked, shocked.

"Whoa, Nancy Weirdo has, like, *two* dates," Trish said.

"That other one is cute," Inga noted, obviously smitten with Ned. "I mean, I don't usually care for the just-back-from-slopping-the-hogs type, but he's cute."

Chinatown was buzzing with its usual excitement as Nancy, Corky, and Ned walked the streets. They stopped at a small café and looked at menus.

"Hello." A waitress greeted them at their table. "Would you like to order some drinks?"

"I'll have a glass of milk, please," Nancy requested.

"Milk!" Corky exclaimed admiringly. "How refreshingly wholesome. I'll have the exact same thing."

Ned looked from Corky to Nancy. "Why is this person here?" he asked her.

"Nancy and I met and things just clicked," Corky replied. "We laugh. We talk. We keep it real. She's my touchstone. We're basically best friends. It's funny, she never mentioned you before."

Ned didn't bother responding. Rather, he turned to the waitress. "Um, can I get an iced latte?" he asked, obviously trying to sound as sophisticated as anyone else in the city.

The waitress barely stifled her giggle. "No latte in Chinese restaurant, silly," she told Ned.

"Yeah, silly," Corky added, echoing the waitress. "No latte in Chinese restaurant."

Ned rolled his eyes. "Don't talk to me, okay?"

"All right," Nancy said, trying to lighten the mood. "Isn't this fun?" She turned to Corky. "You know, Ned and I have known each other since the second grade. He helped me solve the Mystery of the Chalkboard Erasers."

"It was the janitor," Ned revealed.

"Ooh, fantastic," Corky said sarcastically.

Suddenly Inga and Trish appeared as if from out of nowhere. They pulled up two more chairs and joined Nancy and the boys. Inga made sure to wedge herself right between Nancy and Ned.

"Oh my gosh, how funny," Inga cooed. "Here we are, and here you are." She flashed Ned her most flirtatious smile. "Hi! What's your name?"

Ned gulped. "Ned?" he said, making it sound more like a terrified question than an answer.

"You're not sure?" Inga laughed.

"No," Ned replied, clearly flustered. "I mean, yes. Yes. I'm sure."

"Why are you here?" Corky demanded of his sister.

"Why are *you* here?" Inga asked her brother.

Ned seconded that. "Why *are* you here?" he asked Corky.

"Hey, hey, guys, don't gang up on me," Corky replied. "I'm sensitive."

○—

After lunch Nancy did her best to lose Inga and Trish. The last thing she wanted was to have those two along while she was sleuthing. Unfortunately, losing the girls also meant losing Ned and Corky, but it had to be done. And so she ran off while the others were busy dancing to the tunes of a street band.

K. G. Louie's wasn't difficult to find, despite the narrow wandering Chinatown streets. Of course, the big sign above the door helped. Nancy walked right inside and was immediately greeted by the shop's owner, Louie.

"Hello," Nancy said. "I'm looking for a box. That is, one in particular."

"What kind of box?" Louie asked.

Nancy thought for a moment. She had no idea. Except . . . "Chinese?" she asked.

Louie turned, and gestured at the contents of the shop. It was filled with hundreds of Chinese boxes in all shapes and sizes. "You've come to the right place," he told her.

Nancy sighed. This wasn't going to be easy. But then, nothing having to do with this mystery had been easy. She opened her mouth to ask Louie another question, but she was interrupted by a familiar voice.

"So this is why you wanted Chinese food," Ned said, walking up behind her.

Nancy shrugged sheepishly. She'd been caught. And a moment later Corky, Inga, and Trish joined them. There would be no more secret sleuthing. But maybe that wasn't such a bad thing, what with all these boxes and everything.

"Everyone pick a row," Nancy told them. "And check inside each box. We're looking for a will."

Surprisingly, no one questioned her. They simply began looking through the rows and rows of Chinese boxes, searching for the elusive piece of paper. But after searching every box in the room, they came up empty.

Nancy turned to Louie for help. He nodded, as if remembering something long forgotten. "There is one more," he said, leading Nancy and her friends to an ornately carved box decorated with dragons. Nancy took a deep breath and slowly opened the box.

There was nothing inside.

Nancy thanked Louie for his time and headed back toward her roadster. Her disappointment was visible on her face. Ned knew enough to leave her alone when she felt this way, and so he lagged behind, letting her walk to the blue roadster by herself. Corky seemed to follow his lead. But Inga wasn't about to let a little missing will keep her from finding out what she wanted to know. She hurried to keep up with Nancy's quick pace.

"So, Nance," Inga asked, trying to sound chummy, "what's the deal with you and Ned?"

Nancy stopped beside her car and listened for a moment.

"Do you hear something?" she asked Inga.

Inga shrugged. But Nancy was sure she'd heard a ticking noise coming from the backseat of her car. Sure enough, there was a small package, with a timer attached. Without missing a beat, Nancy reached into her sleuth bag and pulled out some wire cutters.

"I mean, are you two, like, a thing?" Inga asked, oblivious that Nancy was now snipping the wires that attached the timer to the package.

"Um, excuse me," Nancy said, pushing Inga slightly to the side. "I think I need to defuse this bomb."

"No kidding," Inga replied, nodding with understanding. "Love is a battlefield."

But Nancy wasn't listening to Inga anymore. Instead she was focusing on the series of beeps coming from the package in her car. She wasn't going to be able to defuse the bomb. There was only one thing to do. She picked up the device, walked over to a sewer hole missing its grate, and tossed the bomb inside.

"Everybody get down!" Nancy called out to the people on the crowded Chinatown street.

*KABOOM!*

A giant fireball blasted out of the ground as the bomb exploded. People began screaming and crying. Panic erupted on the street.

"What was that?" Ned cried out to Nancy.

But she didn't reply. Instead she pulled her camera out of her sleuth kit and snapped a few shots of the large black vehicle that was driving away. "That's the SUV that tried to run us down. The side's damaged. Come on!"

Corky leaped into the roadster and hid in the backseat. Ned and Nancy piled in as well, leaving Inga and Trish behind.

"What was that?" Corky called to the front seat as Nancy sped off after the SUV. "Are you okay? What was that? What was that?"

"Hurry up," Ned urged Nancy. "We're losing them!"

"They turned up that street," Nancy said, pointing to a side street as she weaved back and forth between cars. She turned in the direction of the SUV.

"Hold on a sec," Corky shouted. "I thought we were driving away from them. That's the only reason I got in the car!"

Ned looked back at the panicked twelve-year-old. "Buckled up?" he asked.

Corky bristled angrily. "I'm fine," he declared.

Nancy hung a sharp left. Corky flew across the backseat and let out a shriek. "Buckling up!" he said, and gulped. His face got slightly green and his stomach flipped as Nancy wound through the back alleys of downtown Los Angeles.

"Say we actually *do* catch up with them." Corky said between bouts of nausea. "What happens then?"

"It really gets my goat when someone tries to kill me. It's so rude. It only makes me want to try harder," Nancy complained.

Ned pointed to the gas pedal. "Then let the horses run, sister."

Nancy shook her head. "We will go the posted speed limit and no faster," she insisted.

"Everybody in the universe drives over the speed limit, Nancy," Ned argued.

Corky shook his head. "What Nancy is saying is that the ends do not justify the means," he said with an air of superiority.

"Your means will lose 'em!" Ned shouted at Corky.

"It's important to judge the ends and judge the means independently in order to do what's right," she told both boys.

"Didn't you promise your father that you wouldn't sleuth?" Ned reminded her. "Aren't you breaking that promise? Is that right?"

Nancy took a deep breath, and pulled the roadster to a stop at the next traffic light. "I want to be honest with my father, but I also want to help Jane and her little girl. It's what you call a moral dilemma."

"What are you going to do?" Ned asked her.

"I have to stop," Nancy said, trying to convince herself as well as Ned. "I have to stop and be normal."

And so she sat there stopped at the light, watching sadly as the big black SUV hurtled away.

# CHAPTER 10

On Sunday morning Nancy woke up bright and early, vowing to make good on her promise to be a normal teenager. And when her father came downstairs for breakfast he found her out on the patio, in a beret, with a paintbrush in hand, creating a portrait of Ned and Corky.

"What's this?" Carson asked his daughter.

"Just normal stuff," Nancy told him. "Normal teenage stuff."

"I support your normalcy." Carson applauded her as he took his coffee and walked off toward the room he was using as his office. "Carry on."

"Ouch!" Ned cried out suddenly. "He pinched me."

"Deal with it," Corky told him, refusing to break his pose.

Ned looked at Nancy and shook his head angrily. "If we're going to babysit, then we should get paid," he told her.

Nancy looked over at Ned's disheveled clothing. "Why is your shirt all wrinkled?" she asked him.

"My closet is only six inches deep," Ned explained.

"That's impossible," Nancy said. "How could . . ." She stopped midsentence as a thought formed in her mind. "Show me."

Nancy and Ned raced off the patio and inside.

"Where are you guys going?" Corky called, running after them.

As they hurried up to Ned's room, Corky trailed behind, obviously annoyed at having been forgotten. "Seriously, whenever you feel like letting me know what's going on . . . ," he remarked sarcastically as he watched Nancy push Ned's clothes to the side and run her hands over the brick wall at the back of the narrow closet.

But Nancy did not answer him. Instead she ran out of the room and raced up the attic stairs. When she reached the attic, she focused her attention on a piece of paneling in the wall that seemed just slightly out of place. Quickly the young detective went straight to work pushing and pulling the wood, until suddenly . . . THE WALL OPENED!

Nancy fearlessly peered inside the opening and discovered a built-in ladder that led straight through the center of the house.

"A secret passageway," Ned murmured.

"This is how the intruder has been getting upstairs," Nancy deduced.

"This is nuts!" Corky added.

"Ned, will you get my flashlight?" Nancy asked. "It's in my kit."

Ned nodded and started for the stairs. Then he stopped and looked suspiciously at Nancy. "Wouldn't this be considered sleuthing?" he asked.

Nancy shrugged. "Who are we kidding? I can't stop!" And with that she jumped into the secret passageway. She popped her head out a moment later. "Once I've found the will and determined the identity of Z, then I'll tell my father everything," she promised Ned. "He'll understand. I mean, how else am I going to help Jane find her real family? It's important." She popped back into the passageway, only to stick her head out again a second later. "Don't you think?" she asked.

Ned gave her a reassuring nod, which was all the encouragement Nancy needed. She smiled broadly and then dove right back into the dark, musty, cobweb-framed passage. She climbed slowly down the ladder, feeling her way with her hand, until she touched upon a small lever. She pulled the handle and a door opened. Nancy peered through the doorway. Aha! This entrance was right behind the fireplace that lined the wall of her room. So that was how the intruder had gotten there to steal her moccasins and her Pee-Chee folder!

The ladder continued straight down. Nancy went on climbing through the darkness, feeling her way along the walls as she traveled. A few minutes later she heard Ned's voice calling to her.

"Nancy, where are you?"

"I'm in the basement," Nancy called back. She reached up and caught the flashlight as Ned tossed it down. Now, with a light to help her, Nancy was able to get a better view of what was inside the passageway. Surprisingly, it did not go straight down to the ground. Instead it made a sharp turn.

"Nancy, are you all right?" Ned asked her.

"I've found a tunnel and I'm going in," Nancy called back up. "If I'm not back in ten minutes, it means something bad has happened."

Corky chuckled, but Ned's glance stopped him cold. "I don't think that was a joke," Ned informed him.

The two boys looked at each other nervously. Was Nancy going too far this time?

Nancy had to crouch down to make her way through the tunnel. In the distance she could see a light, but she was unsure where it was coming from. There was only one way to find out, of course. Nancy would have to crawl through the tunnel and discover where it led.

A few minutes later she had her answer. As Nancy climbed out of the tunnel, she came face-to-face with a woman doing laundry. Nancy was no longer in the Draycott mansion. Rather, she'd come out of the tunnel in the apartment building nearby. Someone had built the tunnel to connect the two.

"A tunnel in the laundry room," the woman said aloud, after she'd gotten over the shock of seeing Nancy emerge from the laundry room wall. "What is *that* about?"

"John Leshing is a tenant in this building," Nancy told her. "He's also the caretaker of the Dehlia Draycott estate. If anyone knows about this tunnel, he must."

"That man has always given me the willies," the woman told Nancy. "You know, the drowning-kittens type."

Nancy frowned. The image was very upsetting—especially because she knew exactly what the woman meant.

# CHAPTER 11

Just because Nancy was back to sleuthing again didn't mean she was completely giving up on her quest to be more normal and make some friends in her new high school. So on Monday morning she came to school armed with beautiful handwritten invitations. Each one read:

Dear Friend,
You are cordially invited to attend
a birthday party for Nancy Drew.
Eight p.m., Saturday evening.
Appropriate dress, please. I hope you attend.
Nancy

Inga and Trish were among the first to receive Nancy's invitations. They looked at them curiously. "I know that she's weird," Inga told Trish, "but we have to go."

"Why?"

"Ned, my future husband, will be there," Inga explained.

Trish nodded. Of course. She completely understood.

Nancy's invitations were not limited to kids at Hollywood Hills High. She desperately wanted Jane and Allie to attend the party as well. But when she arrived at Jane's small apartment, the door was sealed shut. A piece of folded paper was taped to the door. Nancy unfolded the note, and read it with surprise, and dismay: ORDER OF EVICTION——L.A. COUNTY SHERIFF.

Jane and her daughter had been thrown out of their apartment. Now they had no place to live. It was so ironic. Jane was the rightful heir to the estate of one of the richest women in Hollywood, and yet she'd been evicted from the tiny apartment she'd been renting. Of course, that was because Nancy hadn't been able to prove that Jane was Dehlia's daughter. At least not yet.

But she was determined to do so, now more than ever.

○━━

By the time Saturday night rolled around, Nancy had planned the perfect birthday party. The dining room table was laden with trays of popcorn balls, pigs in blankets, and canapés. Ned and Corky had hung streamers and balloons on the walls and ceilings in the dining room and living room. The rooms were very festive.

And so was Nancy's lacy party dress and her shoes. She'd pulled out one of her favorite outfits—she and Bess had bought it in one of the dress shops on Main Street in River Heights. Nancy had also managed to get her hair to flip up perfectly at the ends—which to her mind was just right for a birthday hairdo. Yet despite her ready-to-party appearance, Nancy's mood was far from festive.

"What's wrong?" Ned asked, coming over to the living room window where Nancy sat staring out.

"I'm going to set a little trap for Leshing," Nancy whispered to Ned. "I think he knows about the secret passageway and what it's used for. Therefore, he might know the identity of Z." She paused for a minute, thinking. "Unless he's the mystery man himself," she added.

"It's your birthday," Ned reminded her. "Do you ever stop working?"

"No," Nancy told him with a grin. She grabbed him by the hand. "Come on!" she said, pulling him over toward the old-fashioned stereo cabinet in the living room. She took one of Dehlia's old record albums and put it on the turntable. "Downloading's cool," she remarked as she began to dance to the twanging guitar sound of an old sixties band, "but nothing sounds like vinyl."

"You couldn't be more right if you tried, Nancy," Corky agreed, making his way across the floor to dance with her.

Just then Nancy heard the doorbell ring over the music. She danced her way into the hall and opened the door to find Inga, Trish, and a gang of teens standing there.

"I brought a few friends," Inga said. "I hope you don't mind."

"Sure!" Nancy replied cheerfully.

Inga studied Nancy's pretty party dress and flipped-up hair for a moment. "Oh . . . I didn't get the memo about a geek theme," she said, rolling her eyes. Then she caught a glimpse of Ned across the room. "Hey, Ned," she called out, practically bowling Nancy over on her way to him.

○━

After Nancy welcomed her guests and hung up their coats, she promptly left her own party, hurried to her bedroom, and picked up the phone. "Leshing, come quick!" she whispered breathlessly before hanging up the phone. Then she pushed the secret wall in her room back a touch and waited.

But when Mr. Leshing did not arrive, Nancy decided to go and meet him. She moved the secret door a bit farther and stepped into the dark secret passageway, her flashlight in hand. A moment later that light revealed a very angry

Mr. Leshing walking through the secret passage.

"I was just wondering if you knew about the passageway," Nancy told him.

"I think you got your answer," he replied.

Nancy paused for a minute and studied his face. "Are you Z?" she asked him directly.

"Miss Drew, I suggest you join your guests and enjoy your party," he replied, walking back through the passage without answering her question.

Nancy sighed. She was getting close. She could just feel it.

And if she had any doubts of that at all, they ended the minute she returned to the party. Someone was calling her on the phone. And he sounded very angry.

"I warned you, drop this line of inquiry," the man on the other end said in a strong Russian accent.

"Who is this?" Nancy demanded. When there was no response, she slammed the phone down angrily.

Then the phone rang again. "Please stop calling here!" Nancy cried into the receiver.

"Nancy?" inquired the voice from the other end. It was her father.

"Oh. Hi, Dad. Where are you?"

"I'm going to be even later to your party than I thought," Carson explained. "I'm sorry, honey. Is everything all right?"

"Absolutely. Hurry home!" Nancy was anxious to get off the phone and continue solving this mystery, which seemed to be deepening by the minute.

Unfortunately, she wasn't able to concentrate. Inga and Trish's friends were totally out of control. They were throwing their drinks everywhere, slam dancing into the furniture, and fighting with each other. This was definitely not the kind of party Nancy was used to.

"Somebody call 911!" Inga shouted over the din. She turned to Nancy. "You know CPR. Do something. This is not a joke!"

Nancy looked down at the stained carpet. Trish was lying on the ground, flailing around. It appeared she couldn't breathe. But Nancy couldn't be sure. The girls had pulled this trick on her before.

"EMS will be here in ten minutes," some guy called to Inga.

Trish stopped struggling. Her body went limp. Nancy couldn't be sure if it was for real this time, but she couldn't take the chance. The girl wouldn't survive ten minutes. She bent down to the floor, and propped Trish's neck with pillows. "Does she have any food allergies?" Nancy asked Inga.

"She's insanely allergic to peanuts. But she didn't eat anything," Inga told her.

"I had a peanut butter cookie," one of the guys

piped up. "And we were making out."

Nancy listened to Trish's chest. She could hear a heartbeat. "I need a knife or a ballpoint pen," Nancy said. As someone handed a pen to her, Nancy continued, "I'd like to remind everyone that unless you've had advanced emergency first aid training, you must never attempt this on your own." And with that she unscrewed the pen and jabbed it into Trish's neck. A moment later the sound of Trish's breathing could be heard.

○━━

After the emergency services workers carried her friend out of the room, Inga turned to Nancy. "I have to admit that I thought you were, like, an insane freak idiot person before, but you're not. You're terrific!"

"Anyone can learn emergency medical procedures," Nancy informed her.

"No, I'm talking about how great this party was. Saving Trish's life was fantastic also. Anyway, I'd like to take you and your little friend Ned shopping. You really need a decent outfit." She paused for a minute and flashed Nancy a smile. "B.T.W., this is as nice as I get."

Nancy grinned. As she looked around the room at the stained carpet, the spilled food and drinks, and the EMS workers, she saw that she had finally had a typical teenage party. Well, sort of.

"What happened?" Carson asked nervously, stepping through the front door.

"It was a lively party!" Nancy explained to her father. "Almost everyone had a good time."

Just then, the LAPD officer in charge, Sergent Billings, walked into the foyer.

"I take it you're Nancy's father," he said, gesturing to Carson. "We responded to a complaint from a neighbor."

"Dad, this is—"

"No, no, no," Carson interrupted. "Let me say something. You had a wild party. You blew it when Dad was MIA, and things went amuck. I get it. Congratulations! Getting rowdy is part of being a normal nonsleuthing teenager." Carson was proud of his daughter. She was finally experiencing life as a regular teen.

"All right, well, that's a first," Sergeant Billings remarked on his way out.

"Did I mention the emergency tracheotomy?" Nancy added as her dad climbed the stairs to go to bed. He paused for a few moments, and then just kept climbing. Nancy Drew would never be a normal teenager, and he had to learn to make some exceptions.

# CHAPTER 12

Nancy's birthday party marked the last night Ned would be in town. The next morning he had his suitcase packed. He planned to leave after their shopping outing that morning.

After breakfast Nancy, Ned, and Corky followed Inga and Trish into a trendy fashion store.

"Hi," Inga said, marching up to the saleswoman. Inga was furiously texting on her phone at the same time. "Obviously someone here needs some help with her look."

"Oh, it isn't that bad. You're just mixing it up too much. You've got some nice pieces. They're just not working together," the lady responded, commenting on Inga's fashion sense, not Nancy's.

"Me?" Inga screamed in anger, finally looking up from her text messages and staring straight at the saleswoman. "I'm talking about her!" she cried, pointing furiously at Nancy.

"Oh. I'm sorry," the lady said. Then she turned to Nancy. "Hi. Wow, where did you get that dress? It's just darling!"

"I made it, from one of my mother's patterns," Nancy told her.

"I love the sincerity," the woman continued. "I have to take a picture of you. Have you made other pieces?" The saleswoman was very impressed with Nancy's sense of style. Inga, of course, was furious.

○━

Following the outing, it was time for Ned and Nancy to say good-bye.

"I wish you could stay longer," Nancy told him.

"My mom said if I stayed past the weekend, she'd turn my room into a den," Ned joked. He smiled for a moment, but then turned serious. "Nancy, I want you to know that I'm not interested in that Inga person. In fact, she scares me. And if you like that Porky guy—"

"Corky," Nancy corrected him.

"Well, it's all right with me," Ned finished, painfully.

"Ned, he's twelve." Nancy could tell that Ned was jealous, and she was happy to find out how much he cared about her. Nancy took a deep breath, pausing before asking Ned an important question. "Can you tell when a girl looks at you and is thinking how much she likes you and thinking how important it is for you to say how you feel before she says anymore about how she feels about you and other people that you might be jealous of because she's already saying what she feels in her own way?"

Ned looked into her eyes for a moment, not sure what to say. Finally he asked her, "Could you repeat the question, please?"

Nancy sighed. What more could she say? Besides, the taxi had arrived. She hugged him awkwardly. "I'll see you soon," she said. He walked toward the cab, and then he turned and gave her one more longing look before getting in.

Nancy walked back into her house and sadly shut the door. Her mood was cheered slightly, however, when she noticed a package on the table in the front hall. There was a computer-printed note—*Happy Birthday! Love, Dad*—attached to the gift. Quickly Nancy ripped off the bow and wrapping paper and revealed the gift inside. A cell phone! Her very own. Wow! Sometimes normal teenager stuff was pretty awesome!

But Nancy's joy was short-lived. Moments later she heard furious knocking coming from outside. She opened the front door of the mansion and discovered Jane there, crying hysterically. "Are you all right?" Nancy asked.

"No!" Jane sobbed. "Child protective services took Allie. They said I was an unfit mother, but it isn't true!"

A rising tide of fury built up inside Nancy. Jane was a wonderful mother. She didn't deserve this! But this problem was beyond Nancy's ability to solve. She needed the help of someone who always helped people, someone who always put others first.

So that evening when Carson returned home from his law office, Nancy and Jane were waiting for him. Nancy quickly explained to her father that Jane had been wrongly accused of being an unfit mother, and that she needed his aid to get her daughter back.

"I can certainly try," Carson assured her. "You can come downtown with me in the morning, Jane."

"Thank you so much," Jane replied sincerely.

"So what's the connection?" Carson asked Nancy and Jane. "How did you two meet?"

"Oh. I'm Dehlia Draycott's daughter," Jane replied matter-of-factly.

*Oops.* From the look on Carson's face, Nancy knew he'd become suspicious. "Dad, it's so late," she said, trying to ward off the inevitable questions. "Let's go over this in the morning."

But Mr. Drew wasn't so easily dissuaded. "Have you been sleuthing?" he asked his daughter.

"Do you really think I've been sleuthing, Dad?"

"You're not answering my question," Carson said.

"You're not answering mine," Nancy countered.

Carson Drew shook his head in frustration. "I'm going to bed," he said, storming off.

As soon as Mr. Drew was out of the room, Jane leaned forward to confide in Nancy. "I have to tell you something," she whispered. "Right after you first found me, someone came to my apartment, a man, and he told me that if I ever tried to prove that I was Dehlia's daughter, I would regret it."

"What did he look like?" Nancy asked her.

"Big," Jane said. "With dark hair. Scary. With one pale blue eye and one black."

True to his word, Carson Drew began working on Jane's case the very next morning. He went with her to city hall to try to find out what had prompted child protective services to remove Allie. But he came up blank. "Someone is filing grievances against you," he told Jane, "but I don't know who . . . yet."

"It isn't true!" Jane insisted.

"I believe you," Carson assured her. "I think the judge will too. It just takes time. We'll get her back. I promise. Is there anyone who might have something against you?"

*Others first.* The words rang through Nancy's head. She knew her father would be upset when she told him what she'd been up to, but in order to help Jane he would have to know all the facts.

"Dad, look . . . there's something I need to tell you," Nancy began. But before she could get her confession out, someone called out to them.

"Carson! Nancy!"

Nancy turned around to see Dashiel Biedermeyer, the lawyer Nancy had tried to meet with a few weeks before. Nancy looked at him with surprise. What was he doing here? Why would such an important man remember her name?

"After Jane's little revelation, I found out who the lawyer for the estate was and I gave him a call," Nancy's dad explained. "He and I are going to talk something over privately. Do you have your car?"

"Down the block," Nancy replied with a nod. "But—"

"Dinner, tonight," her father promised. "I have a lot of questions and I think you just might have the answers."

Nancy drove Jane back to the Draycott mansion, and together they waited for Carson Drew's return. They hoped he would have good news about Allie, and about Jane's rightful ownership of Dehlia Draycott's estate. Already Jane had become accustomed to the idea that her mother was actually the great actress. It became more and more real as she and Nancy watched her old movies.

"It's so weird. I never thought about her before, but now I see her everywhere," Jane said, staring at the image on the screen. She sighed for a moment. "Maybe I am an unfit mother," she remarked slowly. "I mean, I don't know what I'm doing. No one ever taught me what to do. I don't think you understand what it's like growing up without a mom."

But Nancy did understand. "Actually, my mother died when I was young," she told Jane.

"Oh, I'm sorry," Jane replied sincerely, with tears forming in her eyes. "I didn't know."

Nancy touched the pendant around her neck—the one that had been her mother's.

"Sometimes I think I can remember her," Nancy confided, "but I never know if what I'm remembering is something I saw in a picture or made up. She's a . . . a mystery."

For a moment an uncomfortable silence filled the

room. Nancy was thinking about her mother, and Jane was thinking about her daughter. All that could be heard was the movie dialogue coming from the DVD player. Then something caught Nancy's attention.

"Wait a minute!" Nancy exclaimed suddenly, hearing some familiar words coming from Dehlia's character.

"The will is in the Chinese box."

Nancy stopped and watched the movie carefully as an actor playing an old Chinese priest led Dehlia's character to a Chinese box. The box looked exactly the same as the one with the dragons on it that Nancy had seen that day in Chinatown. "You must make the dragon bow," the actor said, pressing down on an ornamental dragon on the side of the box. Immediately a panel inside the box popped open, revealing the papers inside.

Nancy's head practically exploded with excitement as it all became clear. "I must have fallen asleep and heard this dialogue," she said, as much to herself as to Jane. "Dehlia used a clue from her own movie to show someone where to find the will. Now I just have to make the dragon bow!"

And with that, Nancy raced from the house, leaving Jane confused and alone.

○━

Nancy made it to Chinatown in record time—despite obeying the speed limit and stopping at all the red lights.

When she arrived at K. G. Louie's, she found Louie enjoying his dinner. Luckily, he was more than willing to help her. Once again she followed him to the back of the store, where the Chinese box with the dragon decorations was.

Nancy opened the top of the box and pressed gently on the dragon as she had seen the priest do in the film. The bottom of the box popped open, and sure enough, there was a large envelope hidden inside: THE LAST WILL AND TESTAMENT OF DEHLIA DRAYCOTT.

"It's the will," Nancy said quietly.

"If you want it, you can have it," Louie said.

"Thank you so much," Nancy answered sincerely. She left the shop with the papers clutched in her hand. She didn't dare open them while anyone, not even Louie, was nearby. These had to be kept secret until she could show them to her father and Jane.

Finally Nancy found a deserted alleyway. It was perfectly desolate. She scanned the paper until she found the words she had been seeking:

*I bequeath all my property and assets to my daughter, born July 28, 1981.*

○—

"I knew it!" Nancy exclaimed with delight. She pulled her new cell phone from her bag and dialed her father's work number. He answered a moment later.

"Dad! I have to talk to you. It's about Jane and how we actually met. She's—"

Carson stopped her midsentence. "What number is this?" he asked.

"From a cell phone," Nancy told him. "The one you gave me."

"I didn't give you a cell phone," her father remarked with surprise.

That stopped Nancy dead in her tracks. Then she remembered that the gift her father had gotten her was her blue roadster and Ned—not the phone! No, the phone had been a plant. Someone was using it to track her every move. They probably knew exactly where she was right then.

"Dad, I need to get off the phone," she said quickly. "Everything's fine. I'll see you tonight."

But everything wasn't fine. Not by a long shot. Before Nancy could toss the phone, that same black SUV slid into view.

Two men in dark clothing leaped out and grabbed Nancy from behind. The larger man had a cold, calculating look in his eyes. And those eyes were very frightening, particularly because they were two different colors—one pale blue, and the other black.

# CHAPTER 13

The men must have given me something to make me sleep, like chloroform. That was Nancy's first thought when she awoke. Her second thought was: Where am I?

It was clear the men had dragged Nancy to an old theater somewhere. At the moment she was locked in the projector room with no immediate means of escape. She climbed up on a table and looked through a glass window. From her perch she could see three large men sprawled out on movie theater seats watching an old television that had been set up on a table. Nancy's long-lost Pee-Chee folder and moccasins were on the table as well.

"So they're the ones who've been breaking in!" Nancy deduced angrily.

Nancy wasn't about to let these men get away with breaking and entering, stealing, and kidnapping. Her trained eyes fell on some scaffolding high above the seats where the men were sitting. With a little work, she thought. . . .

Nancy searched her sleuth kit for just the right tools needed to escape the projector room prison she'd been dragged into. And a moment later she had made it through the window above the projector and was climbing along the overhead beams.

From her perch above the theater seats, Nancy spied the most important item of all sitting on the table beside the TV. *Dehlia's will!* The men had taken it from her while she was unconscious. She had to get it back!

Quickly Nancy fashioned a makeshift fishing rod from a paper clip and a piece of string she had in her sleuth kit. Then, with expert precision, she lowered the string over the will and hooked the papers with the clip. Then she reeled them back up to where she was perched.

Talk about the catch of the day! The will was safe in Nancy's hands—for the time being, anyway. Nancy knew that as soon as the men discovered she'd escaped from the projector room, all bets were off.

*Crash!*

That time, apparently, was now. The old scaffolding

had collapsed under Nancy's weight, and she fell to the floor, landing not twenty feet from the hoodlums who'd kidnapped her.

"Excuse me!" Nancy shouted as she ran out of the theater, through a back door, and down a staircase. Unfortunately, the stairs led to a brick wall two stories above the sidewalk below. Jumping would be dangerous. Of course, so would staying put.

Nancy had no choice. She had to jump. She took a deep breath, and felt her feet leave the wall. A moment later she landed—right on top of a mound of garbage that had been loaded into a garbage truck. It was smelly but soft.

A few moments later Nancy found herself back on the streets of Chinatown. She leaped into her blue roadster and sped off in the direction of the Draycott mansion.

Unfortunately, the thugs were on to her. She hadn't driven more than two blocks when that awful big black SUV appeared as if from out of nowhere. The huge car lurched forward and rammed Nancy's roadster, hard. The convertible spun of out control.

"Aaaaaaahhhhhh!" Nancy screamed as her roadster slammed into a row of parked cars.

A half hour later Carson Drew was finally able to locate his daughter among the sea of patients in the hospital emergency room. She had a few cuts and bruises, but from the look of things, Nancy was going to be all right.

"Hi, Dad!" she said, perking up as her dad walked into the room.

"Are you okay?" Carson asked frantically. "What happened?"

Nancy looked at Sergeant Billings, who had come to take the accident report. Then she looked at her father. "It was just your run-of-the-mill car accident. I swerved out of control because . . ." She sighed heavily. This was it. No more lies. The jig was up. "Because men were chasing me," she said honestly. "I've been working on a case."

Sergeant Billings stood. "I'm going to give you two some time," he told the Drews, and walked out of the curtained area where Nancy was being treated.

Carson was obviously fighting to hold back his anger. "You promised you wouldn't do this, Nancy," he said finally.

"I'm sorry, Dad. I was trying to help Jane and Allie. I started to tell you today."

"You could have been killed. Do you realize that?"

Nancy nodded. "I was just trying to do the right thing." She paused for a moment, choosing her words carefully. "I wanted to follow your no-sleuthing rule," she told her father honestly. "But I couldn't do both. It was a moral dilemma."

"This is a dangerous city," Carson reminded his daughter. "The rest of the world is not like River Heights."

"I know that now," Nancy told him as her eyes filled with tears. "I tried to be normal. I really did. I just lose control and start sleuthing, and when I get started working on something, I can't stop."

Carson grinned—but only slightly. "I wonder where you get that from?" he mused.

"I mean, the idea of a girl out there without her mom . . ." Nancy's voice drifted off sadly.

Carson nodded slowly. This case had hit close to home for her.

"Dehlia wanted to leave Jane the estate. And I found the will, which is a good thing. I was just trying to help someone. That's what you always taught me to do. Others first."

Carson sat down beside his daughter and caught his breath as he began to understand the enormity of the night's events. "I just wish you had talked to me about this," he said, taking her hand and fighting back the tears.

"Dad, it'll be okay. We'll work it out," Nancy said, suddenly comforting her father instead of it being the other way around.

Just then someone coughed gently. Mr. Biedermeyer poked his head into the curtained area. "Your father and I were going over some business when we heard," he said, speaking to the surprised look on Nancy's face. "I hope you're all right."

"I'm fine," Nancy assured him.

"He's offered me some consulting work, and I can do it from home," Carson explained to Nancy. "We can go back to River Heights." He leaned in and whispered into his daughter's ear, "And it pays a lot."

"Oh," Nancy answered with a slight grin.

Carson had ridden with Mr. Biedermeyer to the hospital in his limousine, and the wealthy lawyer offered the two Drews a ride back to the Draycott estate. Carson and Nancy sat on one side of the limousine with Mr. Biedermeyer, while another lawyer in a dark suit sat across from them. Carson Drew was busy poring over some legal briefs he was preparing for Mr. Biedermeyer's signature. But the old lawyer seemed more interested in Nancy's case than the work her father was doing.

"I couldn't help but overhear before about the mystery," he remarked to Nancy. "Did you ever find the will?"

"I did! Dehlia used one of her movies as a clue. It was hidden in a secret compartment in a Chinese box."

Carson smiled proudly. "Nancy always gets to the bottom of a case," he boasted to Mr. Biedermeyer.

"My firm would certainly be interested in seeing that will," Mr. Biedermeyer told Nancy enthusiastically. "Where is it now?"

"Mr. Biedermeyer wasn't just Dehlia's lawyer; he was her manager, from the beginning," Carson explained to Nancy. "He made her who she was. He brought her account to his law firm." Carson stopped for a moment and handed some papers to Mr. Biedermeyer for his signature. "Time to sign on the dotted line."

The older lawyer took a pen and scrawled his signature across the bottom of the page. Dashiel Z. Biedermeyer. His middle initial alone took up half the signature line.

"Now, that's quite a signature," Carson Drew remarked.

"My middle initial," Mr. Biedermeyer replied. "For Zachary."

"Z . . . ," Nancy said under her breath. Z. *Like the person mentioned in Dehlia's letter.*

Z was sitting right beside her in the limousine! Her heart began to pound. This seemingly kind old gentleman was not at all who he appeared to be. But there was no way she could tell her father that. Not with Z sitting right there.

"Where's the will?" Mr. Biedermeyer asked her again, a slightly menacing tone barely noticeable in his voice.

"I-I . . . ," Nancy stammered.

"Where is it, honey?" her father asked. "Do you know? Actually, this is a little awkward. His firm stands to lose more than a little income if the money from the will really does go to Jane."

Nancy looked straight ahead as she tried to figure out how to handle this. But how to handle things became abundantly clear when she caught a glimpse of the limo driver's face in the rearview mirror. He had two differently colored eyes: one pale blue and the other black.

"Dad!" Nancy exclaimed. "We have to get out of this car! Now!"

Carson looked at her with surprise. "Why?"

Nancy leaned forward to speak to the driver. "Excuse me, sir, could you please stop the car?"

The driver would do no such thing. That left Nancy with just one choice. She pushed the door open and leaped out of the moving vehicle.

But Carson was not lucky enough to escape. The large man in the dark suit grabbed him and held him prisoner in the car.

"Nancy!" Carson Drew cried out into the night.

"Dad! Get away from them!" Nancy shouted back.

But it was no use. The limo sped off, taking Nancy's father right along with it. She had to get help! Quickly Nancy charged over to a nearby apartment building— the same building that Mr. Leshing lived in. The same building that had a secret tunnel leading straight to Dehlia Draycott's mansion!

Nancy flagged down an elderly woman entering the building with some groceries and somehow managed to convince the woman to allow her to come inside and use the telephone. Nancy dialed the police station—only to be put on hold once again.

"Do you know if a man named Dashiel Biedermeyer ever rented in this building?" Nancy asked the woman, as bad elevator music hummed in her ear through the phone receiver.

"No, no, he owns it," the older woman explained. "He owns that house you're in too. He's a very rich man."

Nancy nodded thoughtfully, and took the phone toward the window. She moved the drapes aside slightly, just far enough to see the black SUV parked outside. Two of Biedermeyer's henchmen were there as well, lying in wait . . . for *her*!

"Is there a back door, please?" Nancy asked nervously.

The older woman pointed toward her kitchen. There was no time to waste. So, despite the fact that she was still on hold with the LAPD, Nancy turned and handed the phone to the woman. "Tell Sergeant Billings to send a car to the house!"

Nancy dodged down the back stairs toward the basement of the apartment building. She was in a real hurry to get to the secret tunnel that would lead her to her own house.

Unfortunately, Nancy and Leshing weren't the only two people who knew about the tunnel. Biedermeyer knew about it too. And he was waiting for her.

"Where's that will?" he demanded, placing his icy hands around Nancy's neck.

"I don't think I should say," Nancy said, keeping her cool as best she could. "It's my insurance that you won't hurt me."

Biedermeyer tightened his grip. "I'll squeeze it out of you!"

"Tell me something first," Nancy said, her curiosity getting the better of her. "Why did you kill Dehlia?"

Biedermeyer didn't even bother to deny his crime. In fact, he seemed oddly nonchalant about it. "After she gave up the baby, she went crazy. She was going to quit the business and run off with that caretaker," he told Nancy, as if justifying the act of murder. "He was the father. Whatever. She was my only client. She was going to fire me. I spent twenty years building up her career. She was going to announce it the night of the party. I got mad. I reacted violently. I felt kind of bad about it for a while, but I'm okay with it now."

Especially since Dehlia was worth more to him dead than alive, Nancy thought ruefully. The actress's mysterious death had turned Dehlia Draycott into an entire industry. And all the money had been going straight into Biedermeyer's pocket—until now.

And then there was the issue of Mr. Leshing. "Leshing is the baby's father?" Nancy asked. "Does he know about the baby?"

"It doesn't matter," Biedermeyer insisted, tightening his grip on the young sleuth. "Now tell me where that will is!"

"It's right here," Nancy said, hopelessly unzipping a secret pouch in her jacket. Slowly she began to pull out the envelope. But as Biedermeyer loosened his grip on her, Nancy kneed him where it would hurt the most! He bent over in agony and Nancy ran off.

For an old man, Mr. Biedermeyer was still pretty quick. By the time Nancy reached the Draycott mansion, he was on her tail—with three of his henchmen right beside him. The four evil men bolted after her, chasing her as far as her bedroom. Nancy tried slamming the door in their faces, but

Biedermeyer stopped her by jamming his foot in the doorway. Then he followed her inside. Nancy was trapped in her own room. And there didn't seem to be any way out.

"Just do it," Biedermeyer ordered his henchmen with a menacing glare as he grabbed the will from Nancy. Then, seeing that none of his men were moving, the older man reached into his own pocket for his gun. He was obviously planning on dealing with this himself.

Nancy shook her head. "If you shoot me, it'll leave all sorts of evidence," she told him coolly. "Very messy."

Biedermeyer considered that for a moment and changed his plans. Once again he wrapped his hands around Nancy's delicate neck.

"Strangulation leaves a traceable handprint," Nancy warned him. "Besides, do you want these gentlemen as witnesses?" she asked, pointing to the three henchmen at the door. "Loyalty aside, what's to say a smart prosecutor won't offer them witness protection?"

At the sight of his henchmen suddenly considering this possibility, Biedermeyer put his hands into his pockets. "What do you suggest?" he asked Nancy.

"The best way to kill me?" Nancy mused. "Hmmm . . . Let me think about that."

"Enough!" Biedermeyer shouted, pulling out his gun. But before he could get a shot out, Nancy's wall swung open and Mr. Leshing emerged from the secret passageway.

"Put the gun down," Mr. Leshing insisted, swinging a heavy metal shovel.

Biedermeyer switched his aim toward the caretaker, but Leshing was quick. He used the shovel to whack the gun away and then slammed Biedermeyer in the head, knocking him to the ground.

The sound of police sirens and the sight of red flashing lights coming through the bedroom window startled the henchmen, and Mr. Biedermeyer. The murderer opened his eyes wide, and looked straight into Mr. Leshing's eyes. The caretaker was standing over him, with the shovel in one hand and Biedermeyer's own gun in the other.

Nancy reached into her sleuth kit and hit the rewind button on her tape recorder. Then she pressed play. "I'll squeeze it out of you," Biedermeyer heard himself say. That was followed by his confession of murder. "After she gave up the baby, she went crazy. . . ."

Biedermeyer groaned angrily. He'd just been hit with the same realization as so many bad guys who'd come before him—he'd been outwitted by Nancy Drew, girl detective.

By Nancy's calculations Mr. Biedermeyer would be spending the rest of his life behind bars. But first he was going to have to face two of the most annoying people in all of Los Angeles—

Just then Inga and Trish arrived. The two teenage girls came bounding up the steps into Nancy's room, walked right past the henchmen in black, and plopped themselves down on the bed.

Inga looked down at the floor and spotted Mr. Biedermeyer, somehow missing the fact that the caretaker was standing over him with a gun and a shovel. "Hi, Mr. Biedermeyer," Inga said perkily. "Inga Veinshtein. I'm in water polo with Courtney, your granddaughter."

Biedermeyer wasn't sure what to say. "Uh, I remember you," he murmured.

Nancy looked over at Trish and Inga and was surprised—but not by their entrance into her room. She was more shocked at what they were wearing. In their long skirts, penny loafers, and flipped hairdos, they looked very much like River Heights girls.

"It's called the New Sincerity," Trish told her.

"Oh my goodness," Nancy exclaimed, in shock. Inga and Trish were wearing outfits styled after her!

"Once again I'm on the forefront," Inga boasted, twirling around like a model. "I see something I think is cute, I start wearing it. And in five seconds it's, like, a total trend." She waved her feet toward the henchmen. "Penny loafer moment!" Then she looked at Nancy. "I need to borrow that coat," she told her.

Nancy nodded, but her attention had already turned back to the issue at hand. "Mr. Leshing, thank you so much," she said sincerely.

"You're welcome, Nancy."

"There's something you need to know," Nancy continued. "It's about Jane. She's your daughter."

The old caretaker's face turned ashen as Nancy told him all about Dehlia's pregnancy, and the baby, and the vicious murderer who had kept it a secret all these years. "I . . . I . . . don't know what to say," Leshing murmured.

"HEY, YOU, WITH THE SHOVEL!" Sergeant Billings's booming voice broke the mood as the police officer stormed into Nancy's room. He turned to Mr. Leshing and drew his gun. "Hey, you, with the shovel."

"Oh, no. No, no, no, no," Nancy corrected him. She pointed down to Mr. Biedermeyer. "It's him. He tried to kill me . . . again."

In a moment Sergeant Billings was reading Biedermeyer his rights as he dragged him down the stairs to the squad car. The lawyer's henchmen were right behind, being led away by other police officers.

Nancy went downstairs with Mr. Leshing, Trish, and Inga.

Her father was the first person she spotted. What a relief!

"I was locked in the trunk of the car," Carson said. He grabbed his daughter close. "What happened? Is everything okay?" he asked.

Nancy nodded, and then watched as Mr. Leshing and Jane walked off into the corner to talk. "Yes," Nancy assured her father. "Everything's just fine."

# CHAPTER 14

The next morning Nancy and her father went down to city hall with Jane. They watched as Allie and her mother were reunited, forever. And then Mr. Leshing walked over, eager to meet his granddaughter for the very first time.

Carson Drew turned to his daughter. "Nancy, I want you to know I appreciate how much courage it took to do the right thing. I'm proud of you."

Nancy smiled at her father. He had no idea how important it was for her to hear those words.

With Dehlia Draycott's rightful heirs now reunited, Nancy and Carson knew it was time to leave Los Angeles.

While Nancy was surprised to realize that she would actually miss Inga, Trish, and Corky—well, at least Corky, anyway—she was anxious to get back to her real life in River Heights. Jane, Allie, and Mr. Leshing were equally ready to begin their *new* lives in the Draycott mansion.

Jane had big plans for the huge estate—and, much to Barbara Barbara's dismay, they did not include renting the building out to the highest bidder. "I'm gonna live here with my kid and anybody else who needs a place," Jane explained to the real estate agent.

"I think maybe you and I should talk this over before you make any—"

But Jane had already made her mind up. "Feel free to leave at any time," she told the real estate agent firmly.

○━

A few weeks later a DVD appeared on Nancy's doorstep in River Heights. The return address was Los Angeles. Nancy popped the disc into her machine and sat back on her comfortable old couch in her small, cozy living room to watch.

The first image Nancy saw was Jane waving happily to the camera. She pointed up to a brand-new sign that had been erected above the Draycott mansion: DRAYCOTT HOUSE: A HOME FOR SINGLE MOTHERS.

Nancy grinned as she watched the footage of Jane,

Allie, and Mr. Leshing playing in the backyard with a group of mothers and their children. Nancy was certain Dehlia Draycott would have been pleased with her daughter's use of her inheritance.

Nancy sighed and leaned back for a moment, playing over those last few months in her head. Then she walked outside to check on how much progress Ned had made working on her roadster. That black SUV had done some serious damage to the blue convertible, but it wasn't anything Ned couldn't fix.

Still, while Ned could fix a car, there was little he could do to fix Nancy's severe case of melancholy. "There it is," he said, eyeing her sad expression as she leaned on the hood of the car and stared off into the distance. "Like clockwork."

"What?" Nancy asked him.

"Postpartum depression. You're sad the case is over."

"That's ridiculous," Nancy argued. "I'm glad it all worked out."

Ned shook his head. "You're only happy when there's trouble. This I know for sure. But that's who you are, and it's all right by me."

Nancy stood up and walked over to him. "Oh, Ned, you're sweet," she said with a grin, leaning toward him. He leaned over and planted a gentle kiss on her lips. They moved apart, both surprised—and pleased—at what had just occurred. It was a life-changing moment for both of them.

And then, just as suddenly, the moment was broken. Mr. Drew poked his head out the front door. "Nancy!" he called out.

"Yes?" Nancy shouted back.

"A phone call," her father replied. "Long distance from Scotland. Something about the Loch Ness monster and missing diamonds."

Nancy gasped with unbridled excitement. "Another case!" she shouted, bounding toward the house, leaving Ned standing alone by the car. He stood there for a moment, watching as she headed off toward the house. That was Nancy, always ready for the next mystery. Of course he wouldn't have had it any other way. After all, solving mysteries was what made Nancy Drew so special.